HOCKEY GIRL

Published in Canada in 2012 by Fitzhenry & Whiteside, 195 Allstate Parkway, Markham,
Ontario L3R 4T8
Published in the United States in 2013 by Fitzhenry & Whiteside, 311 Washington Street,
Brighton, Massachusetts 02135

www.fitzhenry.ca   godwit@fitzhenry.ca
10 9 8 7 6 5 4 3 2 1

Library and Archives Canada Cataloguing in Publication
Hyde, Natalie, 1963-
      Hockey girl / Natalie Hyde.
ISBN 978-1-55455-251-1
      I. Title.
PS8615.Y33H63 2012   jC813'.6   C2012-904074-6

Publisher Cataloging-in-Publication Data (U.S.)
Hyde, Natalie.
    Hockey girl / Natalie Hyde.
[152] p. : cm.
Summary: In a hockey-crazed town that cares more about the boys' hockey teams than
anything else, a group of girls fight for their right to fair and equal ice time and put together
a winning team.
ISBN: 978-1-55455-251-1 (pbk.)
1. Hockey – Juvenile fiction. 2. Sports for girls – Juvenile fiction. I. Title.
[Fic] dc23   PZ7.H934Ho 2012

Fitzhenry & Whiteside acknowledges with thanks the Canada Council for the Arts, and the
Ontario Arts Council for their support of our publishing program. We acknowledge the
financial support of the Government of Canada through the Canada Book Fund (CBF) for
our publishing activities.

  ONTARIO ARTS COUNCIL
CONSEIL DES ARTS DE L'ONTARIO   Canada Council   Conseil des Arts
                                                          for the Arts   du Canada

Cover and interior design by Daniel Choi
Cover photo courtesy of Christie Harkin & Emma Miloff
Manufactured by Friesens Corporation
Manufactured in Altona, MB, Canada in August 2012
Job#**77248**

MIX
Paper from
responsible sources
FSC® C016245

HOCKEY GIRL

Natalie Hyde

Fitzhenry & Whiteside

Acknowledgements

My heartfelt thanks to:

Hockey girls, Kate Harkin, Taylor Lanoue and
Heather Orr, for your patience with my questions and
sharing with me your love of the game.

Hélène Boudreau, for your great comments and
feedback on early drafts.

Christie Harkin, editor extraordinaire, for your
valuable insights and enthusiasm for this story.

The staff at Fitzhenry & Whiteside for all their hard
work behind the scenes.

The Ontario Arts Council for their gracious support
through the Writers' Reserve Grant Program.

And mostly to my family; Craig, Alex, Chelsey,
Nathan, Haley, Mom and Dad for your unfailing love
and confidence in me.

For Haley, who inspires me every day.

one

"Tara! Watch out!" Rachel yelled to me.

A red shirt whizzed by. *Oh no you don't, number 24*, I thought. *You're not going to get away with that.* I raced down the rink after her, breathing hard.

Nobody steals the puck from me on a turnover.

As strange as it sounds, this sort of turnover, I've learned, has nothing to do with the golden-brown pastries from Hannah's Bakery. A turnover in hockey is when you lose the puck to the other team. Or rather, when a red shirt manages to steal it right off your stick while you keep skating, looking like a fool.

So, turnovers from Hannah's Bakery: good.

Turnovers in a Cartwright Roadrunners' hockey game: bad.

And even though it was perfectly legal to steal the puck like that, it still struck me as a dirty, underhanded kind of thing to do. Hockey seemed to be full of sneaky tricks and attacks, like the elbows that would ram into my chest, face, or shoulder when the ref wasn't looking. Not at all like softball, where we had been regional champions three years out of four by *not* playing dirty.

My blades cut into the ice near the boards and made a shower of snow as I tried to stop the momentum of my full-speed charge. Physics, however, was not on my side and I slammed into the back of number 24.

A whistle pierced the icy air.

I cringed. Whistles in hockey were usually bad news.

"Blue—number 45! Body contact!"

Perfect. I had a penalty with only three minutes left in a tie game. Somehow I didn't think that was going to improve our coach's mood. And Coach Santos was pretty miserable at the best of times.

I skated over to the penalty box and plunked myself down on the wooden bench inside. Penalty boxes, I decided, were designed to make you feel humiliated. There was no reason why you couldn't serve your sentence on the team bench. Having to sit in that box, separated from your teammates, reminded me of sitting outside the main office at school. Even if you were really only there to hand in a note, just sitting in those chairs for everyone to see made you feel like a loser.

This was every bit as bad. Actually this was worse because in the seats behind the penalty box were the three clowns that had started this whole stupid idea. And they were enjoying every minute of it.

"Oooh, what I wouldn't give for her to slam into me that way," I heard one of them say, deliberately loud enough for me to hear over the game. It sounded like Braydon Hawes.

My hand tightened into a fist but I didn't turn around.

"If I played hockey with girls, I'd want them to wear less padding. It hides all the good parts," another one said, laughing. Oh, that was undoubtedly Tyler Moore, with his stupid, lopsided grin pasted on his face.

I wasn't going to give them the satisfaction of a reaction. Not like Rachel. She probably would have been up over the glass and pounding the snot out of them by now. But Rachel's temper was legendary, and although I would never tell my best friend that it was the reason we got into so much trouble all the time, she was going to have to learn to get it under control. We couldn't be forming new sports teams every time she answered a dare.

I hadn't paid much attention to the guys last summer when they went jogging past the ball field where we had just finished our softball game. I was still smarting from the fact that the only people who had come to watch us play were Andrea's kid brother and the old guy with asthma who needed to rest while walking his dog. Girls' softball didn't exactly draw a crowd in Cartwright.

The guys had made a big of show of laughing really loudly so we would notice them on the field next to the diamond. I knew two of them. They had gone to my elementary school and were arrogant, the way all jocks are—at least in my experience. The third guy with the dark eyes looked familiar; he was probably in grade 10 with my older brother, Will. Kip something, I think his name was. They must have expected all of us to be ogling them in their shorts and muscle shirts.

But our team wasn't interested in looking at sweaty hockey players doing off-season training. We had just won our semi-final game against the Cougars (or were they the Panthers?) and were celebrating the fact that we were off to the championships. We wouldn't have noticed Ryan Reynolds riding by shirtless on a black stallion after a game like that. (That's a lie. We would have noticed Ryan Reynolds with or without a shirt, but none of these guys was Ryan Reynolds, that's for sure.)

So the Three Stooges had resorted to the lame tactics that guys always resort to when they want attention.

"Hey, gorgeous, how about flexing those pecs again?" Tyler had said.

"Yeah, could you bend over and pick up the ball for me?" Braydon added.

I couldn't stop myself from rolling my eyes.

Hockey players. *Ugh*.

"Just ignore them and they'll go away," I whispered to Rachel. But the red was already creeping up the back of her neck.

"You girls want some real training? You should work out with us." Tyler added some hip thrusting gestures to that statement.

"Come on, Rachel." I tried to pull her away.

"Is anyone *ever* impressed by that?" Rachel asked me, loud enough for them to hear.

"Hey, babe. We're just trying to help. You know, 'cause we play a *real* sport."

That did it. Rachel twisted out of my grip and marched over to them, every Irish gene in her DNA quivering with indignation.

"What? Coasting around the ice padded from head to toe in case the widdle puck hits you?"

Braydon and Tyler stood in front of her, each a good head taller than she was. The other guy didn't come over, but stood quietly in the back, his dark eyes dancing.

Braydon locked his eyes on her. "You wouldn't last five minutes in a game, sweetheart. You'd be begging your momma to take you home."

Looking back, this is where I should have jumped in and dragged Rachel away from the rink rats, even kicking and screaming. If I had done that, then we wouldn't now be committed to playing a sport for a whole season where you can sweat and be freezing cold all at the same time.

In my defense, I did open my mouth to stop her...but nothing came out. Powerless, I listened in dread as the fateful words left her mouth.

"Well, maybe we'll just have to form a hockey team of our own in the off-season and show you how it's played."

Tyler was clearly enjoying this. Thinking back, I suspect he did it on purpose, knowing Rachel would bite.

"Let's see it then. Or are you all talk?"

By this time the rest of our team had walked over. I desperately hoped they could defuse this.

"What's going on?" Sam asked.

Braydon turned Rachel around to face the team and put his arm around her shoulders. She twisted out of his grip and he ducked barely in time to avoid her fist. He backed up, laughing. "Rachel here thinks you girls could learn to play a game of speed and power instead of running around on the grass chasing a kiddie ball."

Sam was having none of that. As catcher she spent more time than most chasing the ball and it was hard work with all that gear on. "I'm sure it wouldn't take long to learn how to chase a little piece of rubber," she said. "It would help pass the winter until we can get down to business on the diamond."

No, no, no! This was heading in the wrong direction.

"Real hockey players would wipe the ice with you ladies," Braydon sneered.

"I don't know about that," Sam replied. "Sounds like a game anyone could play. After all, you losers do."

"You think strapping on some figure skates makes you a hockey player?" Tyler asked.

"No more than you picking up a glove makes you a ball player," Rachel retorted.

"You haven't got the guts," Tyler said to her.

"Watch us," Rachel said.

My head ached. I knew that look on Rachel's face. She was like a pitbull with its eyes locked on a target. She had given her word and now nothing would make her back down. Maybe it came from always competing with three older sisters who were brilliant at everything: sports, school, jobs, boyfriends. Rachel was always trying to prove herself.

Leaving the field, I tried to talk her out of it. "We can't just start up a hockey team, Rach. I know from my brothers playing all these years that all the teams are set by now and all the ice time is spoken for."

Rachel glared at the backs of the guys jogging away. "There's got to be something."

"You know, I think there is a rep team," Andrea said, "because my cousins from Julian Falls have come here to play. They keep bugging me to join the league. I guess Cartwright's team is chronically short of players."

"There you go," Rachel said, hitting my shoulder with the back of her hand. "Problem solved. We need a team to play on, and they need players. I couldn't have planned it better myself."

I groaned. This was not going to end well.

On a mission, she called the coach of the Bantam C team, and roped in enough of us to fill the team roster. She tried to tell me that it would be a good way to get to know some of the other grade nines in our new school, but I wasn't sure that knowing two or three new people would help us in a high school of seven hundred. Still, when Rachel introduced me to Deb and Kayla from the Roadrunners, they seemed happy to have new blood. Some of the girls from our softball team, like Andrea and Grace, were excited to play hockey, but others, myself included, had to be blackmailed.

This was the true danger of having a best friend who is fiercely competitive AND who knows all your secrets. I didn't really believe Rachel would rat me out just to join a team but I let her think that was the reason I agreed to play.

Truth is, I was just tired of being invisible in our house. My dad and two brothers were hockey mad, though neither of the boys had ever managed to crack the elite Hornets AAA team. Even my mother braved the cold arenas to watch them play, as long as she had a hot coffee in her hands. Hockey dominated practically every conversation in our house, and everything was scheduled around games and practices. Maybe if I played, I'd finally understand what all the fuss was about.

Watch us, Rachel had told the guys. Well, they were watching us now. From prime seats behind the penalty box. And so far, I was relieved to say, they hadn't had the pleasure of seeing us humiliated on the ice. If we could get one more goal, it would be our second win in only three games. It was probably a combination of the fact that floor hockey was part of our gym course at school so we knew the basics of the game, plus the fact that we had played together as a softball team for so long we could almost read each other's thoughts.

It didn't hurt either that every person in Cartwright, young or old, knew how to skate. Just as people living in the Rockies strapped on skis before they could walk, kids in Cartwright laced up and hit the ponds, the arena, and even the frozen Nith River as soon as they could toddle.

All in all, we made a pretty fair hockey team for mostly first-timers.

We'd probably be even better if I didn't keep getting stupid penalties.

It felt like an eternity for this one to count down, especially as our team was having trouble getting the puck out of our own end.

One minute, forty seconds left in the penalty. I watched a red shirt (I could never remember team names; were they the Hurricanes? Eagles? Earwigs?) take a shot on our net, but it was deflected by Sam's stick. For a second I worried that Sam was going to leave the crease and chase after the puck like she does when she plays catcher. Sam sometimes forgets which game she's playing.

One minute and seventeen seconds still to go. Rachel managed to get her stick on the puck and send it down the ice into the other team's end. I watched from the penalty box as the red shirts skated past me and regrouped behind their net before beginning a new attack down the ice.

Fifty-eight seconds left. There was a scuffle behind our net while everyone fought for the puck. This time it was Lilly from our team who sent it down this way.

Thirty-two seconds. I watched Rachel follow the puck into the red shirts' end and swing her stick in wide arcs, trying to prevent a pass.

Fifteen seconds. The puck was back in our end and the red shirts were trying to shoot on Sam again.

Eight seconds. I stood up, snapped my helmet strap, and put on my gloves.

Three seconds. I put one knee over the door and watched the clock.

Zero. I hopped over the boards and rapped my stick on the ice as a signal to Rachel. She got a hold of the puck and shot it right to me. I was waiting just outside the other team's blue line and there was a satisfying *thwack* as the puck made contact with my stick. I took off into enemy territory. It was just me and the goalie.

I skated in fast and made like I was going to shoot glove-side. The goalie dove to the left and I flicked it to the right.

SCORE!!

My teammates skated over to me and thumped me on the back.

Take that *you goons!* I thought, imagining with satisfaction the three guys with the big mouths in the stands. That should shut them up for a while.

When the buzzer signalled the end of the game, I looked up at the row behind the penalty box, expecting to see the three of them slumped in their seats, mad that, so far, they were wrong about us. But they were on their feet, clapping and cheering. A standing ovation.

Guys.

I'm sure I'll never figure them out.

two

I stood in line at Hannah's Bakery with Rachel the next morning, desperate to satisfy my lingering craving for an apple turnover. It wasn't even eight-thirty and already the line snaked across the front of the shop and almost out the door. Dolores was a blur behind the counter, running from the coffee pot to the display case and back again. Early mornings and right before hockey practices were her busiest times.

"So, why isn't this called 'Dolores's Bakery,'" Rachel asked, fidgeting in line. If we didn't get served soon, we were going to be late for class.

"You weren't here then, but when Hannah Holzhacker sold the bakery to her, Dolores did change the name. She even ordered a new carved sign for out front." We both took a step forward. "But every time she answered the phone with 'Hello, Dolores's Bakery' they would ask for Hannah's Bakery. She would tell them that it *was* Hannah's Bakery, and they would say, 'Well, why didn't you say so in the first place?' It got so confusing that Dolores cancelled the order for the new sign and decided to just keep the old name."

I stepped up to the counter. "One apple turnover and one small hot chocolate to go, please, Dolores."

"Make that two of each," Rachel said.

"I wish I was still young like you and could eat turnovers without them going straight to my hips," Dolores sighed. "But I guess even you girls have to be careful now the season is over, eh? No more softball games to burn off the calories."

I bit into the corner of my turnover. "We're doing a new kind of off-season training this year," I said, a shower of crumbs landing on the front of my hoodie.

"Oh yeah, what's that?" Dolores asked as she rang in the order.

"We've joined the girl's rep hockey team."

Dolores looked up at us. "You're joking, right?"

"No," I said, handing her my money. "Why would we be joking?"

Dolores shook her head as she handed me the change. "With the way the figure skating club had to fight for ice time from the Arena Board, I'm surprised they fit a girls' team into the schedule."

"Well, we don't have the best game times," Rachel admitted.

Dolores made a face. "Just wait until the season really gets started. The men will be trying to hog all the slots for their future NHL stars, just you wait and see. You'll be lucky to play at midnight on a Tuesday."

Dolores got Rachel's order ready.

"Hey, Dolores. Where's George?" I asked. Her husband was usually standing over one of the stainless steel tables at the back, kneading, pounding, or rolling something. Flour dust always settled on his jet black hair making him look like a 'before' ad for men's hair colouring.

"Oh, he's out picking up the equipment for his new business. I told him we don't need another business, I'm busy enough. He should be spending his time dunking donuts in sprinkles, not picking up a new toy." She shook her head.

"What kind of business?" I asked.

"T-shirts. He's gonna put slogans and pictures on them. Even do custom orders."

"That sounds great!" Rachel said. "I want one that says: *When God made man, She was only joking.*"

Dolores laughed. "Sure thing. What about you, Tara?"

"I think I'll stick to a picture," I said. "We're not allowed to wear T-shirts with slogans in school, anyway."

"Oh, shoot, I forgot," Rachel said.

"What's up with that?" Dolores asked.

"Principal Tuttle got mad when someone had a shirt on with a saying he didn't understand. Something like: *There are only 10 kinds of people in the world that understand binary code. Those that do and those that don't.*"

Dolores looked confused for a moment and then brightened. "Oh, I get it now—binary code where everything is written in 1's and 0's? Isn't "one zero" how you write the number two? That's a hoot! Strange that Mr. Tuttle didn't get it."

"Well, if he *did* get it, he didn't think it was funny. He made the school council change the dress code the very next week. No words of any kind are allowed on clothing in school."

"Except, of course," Rachel said, "for the hockey team logos."

We all rolled our eyes. Hockey teams were *always* the exception.

"Well, good luck with your team. I'm glad they're letting the girls play. Maybe the men of this town are finally coming around."

We grabbed our stuff and squeezed through the crowd blocking the door.

I left the shop feeling a little uneasy. Was Dolores right? Was there trouble brewing? We hadn't really faced any problems getting onto the Bantam team—in fact the coach seemed to jump at the idea. And we had no trouble finding equipment; every house in Cartwright has outgrown hockey pads and helmets and gloves somewhere in the garage or basement.

Maybe Dolores was exaggerating. But then, when I thought about it some more, Coach Santos was a bit of a nut job—though I guess, when you need a coach badly enough, beggars can't be choosers. We hadn't really been too concerned about that when we signed up; we were only interested in proving the guys wrong. But now I wondered. Maybe it had all been too easy.

three

I barely had the strength to hang my jacket in my locker. Our practice had been at 5 am which meant I had crawled out of bed at 4:15. I am not a pretty sight that early in the morning: my eyes are puffy, my hair looks like a pack of rats have been nesting in it, and my joints are so stiff that I walk funny. When I first came downstairs I looked like I'd walked straight out of a movie trailer from *The Zombies Rise Again*.

Coach Santos had worked us pretty hard at the rink, barking that he wanted to see us sweat. I don't think we stopped moving the whole hour. By the time we were done I felt like overcooked spaghetti.

I tried to pull my books out of my locker but they felt like they weighed a ton. I wondered how many I could leave behind and still keep up with class. It didn't help that I hadn't eaten yet, but really, who is hungry at 5 am? Maybe some sugar would kick-start my system.

I rummaged around in the bottom of my knapsack for anything edible. Lilly opened her locker two doors down from mine. I pulled out a slightly mangled nutrition bar my dad must have thrown in on one of his parenting-on-the-run days.

"That's *it*, Tara!" Lilly yelled so loudly that I jumped and slammed my elbow into my locker door.

Here it comes, I thought, rubbing my arm.

"That's a great idea! The victim ingests a lethal dose of potassium from nutrition bars. Too much potassium can cause cardiac arrest, you know."

I didn't know. I wasn't sure I wanted to know. But I knew she was going to tell me anyway. Lilly is writing the World's Greatest Murder Mystery. She's been at it for three years now. She is convinced that the only thing standing between her and an Agatha Award is finding the perfect, unsolvable murder.

"How many bars would it take to eat a lethal dose of potassium?" I had to ask. I shouldn't encourage her madness, I know, but maybe I could use it as ammunition the next time my dad got on one of his fitness kicks.

"I'm not sure. I'll have to look it up. But no one would suspect a nutrition bar, would they?" she asked triumphantly, as if daring me to come up with a name of someone who would think to kill with health food.

"Nope," I said, tearing off the wrapper and biting off the end. I was totally willing to risk death by vitamins, minerals or whatever, I was that hungry after practice.

"See you in English," Lilly said as she disappeared into

the river of teenagers pushing and prodding each other down the hallway.

I always felt like a salmon swimming upstream as I went against the current of students flowing in the opposite direction. There is only one thing that can part the flow at John Cabot High School, and that's the black jacket with the Cartwright Hornets AAA logo. It's the ultimate status symbol. I wasn't always sure if guys were trying out for the teams so they could play hockey or just get the perks that came with wearing the jackets.

A group of black jackets was passing my locker just as I tried to merge into traffic. I managed to skim along beside them until a hefty shove from a student trying to navigate the hall at a run sent me flying. I slammed into the left shoulder of one of them.

"Whoa!" a voice said. Our eyes locked. It was Kip what's-his-name with the dark eyes.

"Well. If it isn't hockey girl," he said.

I gritted my teeth.

"I thought you gals weren't allowed to check?" This earned him some chuckles from his buddies.

"It seems you guys have a lot to learn about us 'gals,'" I said as I straightened the notebooks in my arms and tried to look unflustered. "We're sorry we've forgotten to—how did you put it?—*beg our mommas* to take us home from the game. I guess we were too busy whupping the other team's butts."

All that earned me was a big grin. "Game's got you, hasn't it?" he said.

What was this? The game didn't 'have' us. We were

only playing to prove a point. And get a little training. We would finish the season but only because we had made a commitment to the league. After that, it was back to our real love—softball. We had some unfinished business with the Hawks who stole the Provincial title from us in the finals.

"The offer still stands for you gals to train with us."

I glanced at him sideways as I peeled away from the black jackets to head to science. Was it a serious offer or was he just yanking my chain again?

"I can't wait to show you my moves." He wiggled his eyebrows.

Hockey players.

four

The mood in the dressing room was upbeat. We heard that our competition tonight was one of the top teams in the league. We always looked forward to playing the good teams in softball; they always brought out the best in us. Maybe hockey would be the same.

The noise in the room was deafening, but over it all I heard Rachel.

"Oh, *puh-leeze*, Sam. Do we have to go through this at every hockey game as well as every softball game?"

"Shhh," Sam said, her eyes closed. "I'm channelling."

All of Sam's goalie gear was laid out on the floor in order. It looked like a mini art attack. Slowly, methodically, she began putting on her stuff, left side first. She did the same thing with her catcher's gear before every inning. And curses to anyone who accidentally knocked something out of place on the ground. Sam would take everything off, straighten the gear and start all over again. We were always stressed out that she wouldn't get ready in time.

It was bad enough with softball gear, but Sam's superstitions were causing real problems now that she had so much more to put on. And there wasn't a lot of room on the floor to spread everything out. The first couple of games, it took two or three tries for her to get dressed with everyone stepping on or moving her stuff.

"Come on, Sam." Rachel said. "Coach is waiting out in the hall. He wants to come in and talk to us."

A grunt was the only answer Sam gave.

"I saw the convener out there with Coach Santos. What do you think they were talking about?" Andrea asked. "I thought the two of them weren't speaking to each other after that whole fiasco with the midget team."

"You mean when Coach Santos made the whole team stay in their gear, skates and all, on the bus ride home from the game in Strassburg?" Lilly asked. "I heard about that. Mike Chu's parents were furious. They blamed Coach Santos for Mike's asthma attack that night."

"You don't get asthma from sweaty gear," I said.

"Tell that to the Chus. They demanded Coach Santos be fired." Lilly said.

"Is that why he stepped down?" Rachel asked. "So he could say he resigned instead of being fired?"

Lilly shrugged.

After three attempts, Sam was finally dressed enough for Coach Santos to come in.

"Decent!" Lilly called, opening the dressing room door a crack.

Coach Santos strode in, looking unhappy. He didn't

waste any time getting down to business. "OK, team, our house guests are heavy duty upfront, but they're weak on the D. So let's nix the sin bin, go deep into their backyard, and put the biscuit in the basket."

He clapped his hands and went out to the bench.

There was silence in the dressing room.

Finally Sam spoke. "Was that English?"

"They call the puck a biscuit?" Andrea asked. "What a stupid name."

"I don't know," Jenna said, "My Gran's biscuits are that hard. And sometimes that colour, too. We think she learned to cook in a coal factory. Everything that comes out of her kitchen is black, hard, burnt, or dry."

I didn't laugh. I had gone for dinner at her Gran's once. I think I chipped a tooth on her gravy.

I stepped on the ice and took a couple of turns around our end while Sam roughed up the area in front of the net.

A whistle blew and we took our positions around centre ice. I was shoulder to shoulder with a girl from the other team at the edge of the circle. She had to be twice my size. We watched the two centres focus on the puck in the ref's hand.

Their sticks clashed as the puck dropped and the battle was on.

The other team, I think they were the Cobras, had earned their reputation. They controlled the puck that whole first period while all we could do was chase them around the rink. It was pretty embarrassing. They were up two goals by the end of the first period. I was only grateful that the Three Stooges weren't sitting in the stands watching this game. In fact, the place was almost totally empty except for Grace and Andrea's moms and some parents from the other team.

I did notice that Coach Santos kept glancing up into the seats, and when I followed his gaze I saw three men in expensive-looking suits leaning against the railing.

"Who are they?" I asked Kayla when we were back on the bench.

"I think that's the boys' hockey league convener and two other league bigwigs."

I wondered—*Why were they watching our game?*

"OK," Coach Santos bellowed at the first intermission, standing at the end of the bench. "I want to see some effort out there! I want to see some sweat out there! You've been bouncing around on the ice like baboons! Get your act together! You're making me look like a fool!" He grabbed the nearest towel and flung it in disgust. The towel was too light to go very far and got caught on the edge of the glass where it hung pathetically like a flag of surrender.

We stood there silent. That was unnecessary. No one had to tell us that we had to step it up. We hadn't reached the provincial softball championships three years in a row by lying down and giving up when things got rough.

"Nothing like getting some support from your coach," Andrea said bitterly, skating out onto the ice.

Throughout the rest of the second period, Coach Santos looked tense and distracted. When he wasn't swearing under his breath, he was looking across the ice and up at the three suits leaning on the rail.

We weren't doing too badly. We still weren't handling the puck too well but we seemed to be out-skating them.

Then Lilly made a bad pass up the middle in our own end. *Ouch.* Sure enough, a yellow shirt nabbed the puck and flicked it in a high, floating arch over the defencemen's heads, toward the net. Luckily Sam was on her game. In one fluid movement she dropped her stick and blocker, flicked off her helmet, and caught the puck in her glove as easily as if she were catching a pop-up behind the plate. Then she reached into the glove to take the puck. She lunged forward and made a beautiful throw down the ice to Rachel who caught it, dropped it, and started skating.

The whistle blew.

The ref was making so many arm signals that she looked like she was doing an angry version of tai chi.

"Delay of game! Hand pass!" She skated over to Sam. "You can't take your helmet off during a game! And there's no throwing the puck when you're out of your crease! What were you thinking?"

"Sorry, ref. Force of habit." Sam blushed a little.

On the bench, Mr. Santos threw his hands up in the air and swore again.

I skated over to Sam and tapped her pad with my stick.

"Nice play, Sam," I said. "Just wrong sport."

"This is really going to mess up my game next summer, you know that?"

five

Coach Santos practically ripped the door off the dressing room when he entered during the flood after the second period. I could sense he was not about to give us a pep talk.

"I have never seen such a lack of commitment in my life!" He started as soon as he walked in. "You're letting the other team control the puck. You've got sloppy passing and no speed. And they're outshooting us seventeen to nine. Get your heads in the game! I don't coach losers!" He threw his clipboard into the corner and it clattered to the ground.

There were mumbles from around the room after he left.

"Boy, I would love to test out the perfect murder on *him*," Lilly said as she re-laced her skates. "But maybe iocaine powder is too quick a death."

"Iocaine powder? I thought you were killing with a potassium overdose?" I said.

"Oh, I dropped that idea. I calculated that you would have to eat about a thousand nutrition bars to get a lethal dose. I didn't figure I could get that by the victim."

"Well, no," Andrea said, "they might get suspicious around, oh, bar number three hundred."

Lilly ignored her sarcasm. "So, I came up with the perfect poison. Iocaine powder. It's odourless and tasteless."

"And fictional," Rachel said.

"What?"

"You learned about it from a movie, didn't you?" Rachel asked.

"Well, yeah. But I thought..."

"They made it up."

"Oh." Lilly said, her shoulders sagging.

"What you want is saxitoxin," Rachel went on, "a potent neurotoxin that causes paralysis so the victim suffocates."

The room went silent.

"Where on earth would you get that information?" I asked.

"The more important question is: *why* would she have that information," Andrea said, looking worried.

"Don't you guys ever watch the Discovery Channel?" Rachel asked, shaking her head.

Lilly had perked up. "Cool. So, can I use that in my book?" she asked.

Rachel shrugged. "Be my guest. It's a good thing we

don't have a vial here now. I might be tempted to take it rather than go back out there."

I had to agree with her. This was not what we had in mind when we started this whole little adventure in winter sports.

"I think maybe Coach Santos is getting a little too wrapped up in this," I said. "I don't know about you guys, but I'm not out to win any provincial titles in hockey. I just want to stay fit and sharp until softball season. And make those guys stuff their chauvinistic attitudes."

Heads nodded in agreement.

"And I think things are about to turn around."

"That's just wishful thinking," Jenna said gloomily. "They've outplayed us both periods."

"True," I said, "but their lack of training is starting to show. They look a bit tired to me. We're at our peak right now, after a whole summer of playing ball. If we step it up this period, we could turn this into a whole different game."

We tramped back out to the rink. The puck dropped for the third period. Rachel and I watched from the bench as Andrea's line stole the puck from the other team and took off down the ice. A couple of nice passes and a flick of the wrist put it in the net.

"Woohoo!" I yelled. I glanced over at our coach, but it seemed that even a goal didn't earn us a smile.

The clock was ticking down and we only had about another ten minutes to pour it on. The yellow shirts were struggling to keep up with us as Rachel, Lilly, and I raced down the ice, three on two. Rachel passed the puck to me and I swung my stick back to shoot. Unfortunately, I had left the puck behind and there was nothing on my stick. But on the upside, Lilly had come in behind me, and as the players and goalie were trying to deflect my phantom puck, she took the real one and got it under the pads of the netminder to tie the game.

Coach Santos didn't so much as raise his eyebrows. Really, what would it take to see some enthusiasm in him? Certainly not a tied game, which gave us one point instead of none. The only thing he said to us after the game was, "Practice. Tomorrow morning, 5 am sharp. Everyone there. No excuses."

Then, like the drama queen he was, he exited the dressing room after slamming the door against the wall.

We all breathed a sigh of relief when he was gone.

Were all hockey coaches like that? Our softball coach, Mr. Diegan, was pretty laid back. He knew that a few well-placed comments, about both the good and the bad, worked much better on us than a constant barrage of verbal abuse.

"Was it my imagination," Rachel asked us, "or was Coach Santos grumpier than usual?"

"I think it has something to do with the suits standing up on the rail," Jenna said. "He was watching them more than the game."

"Why do you think they were here?" Rachel asked.

"I dunno. But I got a funny feeling."

We were all quiet. Jenna's 'funny feelings' were never wrong.

six

"Who needs curly fries?" I asked when we were all finally changed and heading out of the arena. My stomach was aching with hunger and it was still at least two hours until supper. Everyone except Andrea, who had to babysit her younger sister while her parents went out, headed to the Burger Bar.

The greasy little diner was *the* hangout for anyone not worried about cholesterol, diabetes, heart disease, or obesity. Those that were went to Wanda's Wheat Grass and More to sit at the bamboo counter and drink sludge that came in a bizarre range of colours. I wouldn't set foot in the place. I'm not eating or drinking anything with ingredients that normal people weed out of their gardens.

The Burger Bar had been in Cartwright forever and was only a block from the arena, so it was always packed before and after games. It was actually named the Burger

Barn, but the tornado of '78 had ripped off the end of the sign, taking the 'n' with it and no one had bothered to fix it.

It didn't seem to matter what the sign read; people came for the food. Some said the smell of fried onions and bacon fat lured customers in from as far away as Julian Falls. If the tables were all full, which happened more often than you'd think, it was possible to get take out.

Every now and then the 'Wheaties', which is what we called Wanda's customers, would try and get the health department to shut down the ancient burger joint. I think they thought they were doing people a favour, saving them from their unhealthy urges. They never succeeded. The health inspector would inevitably be seen leaving the shop, tucking a white paper bag with grease stains on it into his car.

A blast of warm air hit me as I opened the door. I sniffed. A hint of cinnamon. That could only mean apple pie was the dessert special. I hoped I wasn't drooling.

"I never truly appreciated the genius of the 'Parking Lot' before," Rachel said as she dropped her bulky hockey bag onto the shelves near the door with a thud.

I had to agree as I dropped my bag beside hers. In no time the shelves were full of our stuff. Before the Parking Lot, players would put their huge hockey bags on the floor near the tables, making it nearly impossible for the waitresses to try and get around without tripping and spilling everything.

So out of necessity the owner banged two wide, solid

wood planks to the wall by the door. Over them he hung a sign he found on the curb after the snow melted: 'Two Hour Parking Only'. The Parking Lot was born.

"If we pool our money, maybe we can get three orders of extra large curly fries and split them," Sam said, frowning at the coins in her hand.

The door opened and another group of kids walked in with sports bags. Looked like the tyke house-league team coming back from a practice.

"I've got enough for a pitcher of pop, too," I said, pulling out some babysitting money.

We were just digging into the golden-brown piles of fries when the door opened again, sending a blast of cold air our way.

"Uh oh," Rachel said. "Rodent alert."

A whole pack of Cartwright Hornets had come in, flashing their matching jackets, but not carrying any hockey bags. It was a good thing. The Parking Lot was jammed already, and so was the diner. It was just our luck that one of the only booths still empty was right behind ours. I hunched over, hoping they wouldn't see us. At least they hadn't been at the game.

"Well, look here, guys," a voice behind me said. "I believe I've found some Roadrunners."

"*Meep! Meep!*" someone else said, sending the rest of the group into peals of laughter.

Really? Cartoon sound effects?

All we wanted was to eat our fries and have fun, and here they were again. I turned around to tell them to shove off but found myself glaring into with a pair of dark eyes. I didn't expect to be inches from a face. A cute face, at that. I swallowed hard—but only because I wanted to be ready to fire off an insult or two.

He was grinning, no doubt enjoying my discomfort.

I forgot what I was going to say and turned back around, my face growing warm.

I felt someone tapping on my left shoulder. It had to be him; he was the only one close enough.

I ignored him.

The tapping got harder.

All the other girls were staring at me. How I wished I had never mentioned fries and had just gone home.

Now with the tapping was some throat-clearing. "Ahem, excuse me," Dark Eyes said.

"What. Do. You. Want." I said, icicles dripping off every word.

"Do you, um, own the dark blue sports bag with a crest thingy on the side?"

What, was he stalking me now?

"Yes."

"Well, I think someone just walked off with it."

I jumped up and scanned the Parking Lot. The tyke team had dumped their gear on top of ours and the wall by the door was a sea of bags. The white crest on the side of my bag usually made it easier to spot, but now I couldn't see it.

"Crap!" I grabbed my purse and a handful of fries. "I gotta chase down my bag. See you guys tomorrow!" I said to everyone at my table.

"There goes a Roadrunner! *Meep! Meep!*"

Yeah, that was getting old already.

I bolted out the door and looked up and down Water Street. Nothing. What was I going to do now? I had a practice in the morning and no gear.

"I don't think you'll see it. I saw the guy get in a truck with his dad and drive off."

It was Dark Eyes. Still grinning. My eyes narrowed. Was he behind this? Had he gotten some pal to take it?

"How do you know they got in a truck? Hm? And how did you know it was my bag?" I had seen enough crime shows to know that it was the little details that unravelled a story.

He seemed to blush a little. Oh yeah, I had him now. "I noticed the crest when you were carrying it out after your game."

"You were at the game?"

"I was doing a bit of training while my dad…while I waited for my dad." He smiled again. "Nice comeback, by the way. And that was a sweet drop pass for the tying goal."

"What? Oh, er, thanks," I said. He must have meant when I left the puck behind me and Lilly picked it up and scored. There was no way that I was going to tell him that that play was an accident. If he wanted to think that we were that good, he was welcome to. "Do you have any idea who the kid was who took my bag? I have a practice in the morning."

"I know the coach of the tyke team and I'm sure I can find out who the kid is. I'll give you a call as soon as I track it down." He paused and seemed to blush again. "I'll need your number."

Oh, right. Like that was going to happen: I could just imagine my number being passed around all the guys on the Hornets team. Prank calls, graffiti on the bathroom walls at school; the possibilities for humiliation were endless. No thanks.

"How about *I* call you?"

He grinned. "Sure."

I found a pen and an old receipt in my purse and took down his number.

"Give me a couple of hours to track him down before you call, OK?" he said.

What did he think I was going to do? Run home and sit by the phone, waiting breathlessly to call him like some hockey groupie? If I didn't have a practice in the morning, I wouldn't be calling him till I was good and ready.

Well, if nothing else, the walk home was a lot easier without that heavy bag. Rachel's mom would have given me a ride home from the Burger Bar if I had waited, but I certainly didn't want to have to explain to everyone what had happened and how and why I had Kip what's-his-name's phone number.

seven

Dinner conversation at my house was totally predictable. There were three topics, which were usually discussed simultaneously: the weather, the antics of our crazy relatives, and sports. Mainly hockey.

Tonight was no different.

"Did you hear Aunt Patty's Tim is dropping out of school to start a business designing pet clothes?" my younger brother Stephan said, reaching for a roll.

"Speaking of clothes, I want the three of you in jackets tomorrow," my mom said, pointing her empty fork at my two brothers and me in turn. "The wind chill is dropping the temperature below freezing."

"I think he's even going to make doggy underwear," Stephan said, grinning.

"I'm not running any of you to the doctor's with walking pneumonia this year. Right, Bill?"

"Huh? Oh, right. You'll miss half the season with pneumonia. Wear your jackets," my dad said.

Mom rolled her eyes.

"Aunt Patty said that once his doggy line is going, Tim will branch out into other pet clothes."

"My science teacher says that's an old wives' tale," Will chimed in. At sixteen, he was at the age where he liked to argue about everything. "He says you catch pneumonia from germs not from getting cold."

"Your teacher doesn't have to pay for the antibiotics," my mother snapped. "Or lose two weeks sleep listening to you cough all night." She glanced at my dad, giving that warning look that said she was about to be mad at him if he didn't speak up soon.

Dad looked sternly at Will and Stephan. "That's right. You guys won't earn any league points by sitting in the stands."

"Tim wants to make swimwear for ferrets," Stephan said.

"Bill," my mother said, exasperated, "I'm not concerned with who is top scorer in the hockey league. It's more serious than that."

Dad nodded. "Your mother is right. The triple-A scouts can't see how good you are if you're on the bench."

My mother closed her eyes and took a deep breath.

Dad sensed he was missing something. "And there's no refund on registration fees for missing games due to sickness."

Mom covered her face with her hands.

"Aunt Patty says that Tim's pet sports team jerseys are

going to blow the lid off the market," Stephan said.

"My science teacher also says that you don't get cramps by swimming right after eating, either," Will added.

"She says every pet in town will be wearing a Cartwright Hornets' sweater by Christmas."

I looked at our cat, Dusty, who was just sauntering past the table. "I think I'll get Dusty a Roadrunners' jersey for Christmas," I said. "She'd look good in white and blue." The conversation stopped dead. I suspect that everyone had forgotten I was even there.

"Who are the Roadrunners?" Stephan asked me.

"Our hockey team," I answered, a little miffed. He was all about hockey and could rhyme off every team in the area—except his own sister's, apparently.

"I thought you girls were just doing a few exhibition games or something," my dad said.

"Where'd you get that idea?" I was getting a bit angry now.

"I thought I heard someone saying something about the ice time being in short supply," Dad said.

I shook my head. "Coach Santos signed us up for the whole season. We're part of the Western Girls Hockey League—C Division. We're doing great, by the way."

"Well, great for a *girls'* team," Stephan said, rolling his eyes.

Everyone kind of chuckled. I tried to keep my anger in check. I don't have Rachel's explosive temper; mine simmers and churns until finally it erupts in a maniacal rage. My brothers tease me that when I finally blow; they have to think back over three weeks to figure out why I'm even angry.

"So, your team seems to be coming together, Steph," my dad was saying. "How many points out of first place are you?"

"Only four. A good weekend and we'll be back on top."

Dad punched Steph good-naturedly on the shoulder.

"We tied today," I said, moving my shoulder ever so slightly forward for my own punch.

"Tied what?" Will asked.

"Our game," I said. "I made a sweet drop pass for the tying goal."

Will snorted. "It was probably an accident. Are you sure you didn't just leave the puck behind?" That earned him a few chuckles.

I looked down at my plate and hoped I wasn't blushing.

"Did you put your gear out to dry, Tara?" my mom asked. "My laundry room already smells like an old locker room. There's probably fungus everywhere in that gear."

Mom lived to disinfect. She had the world's most sensitive nose and I swear she could detect a single spore of mold in an open field. If she had her way, every piece of hockey gear in Cartwright would be soaked in bleach every night. All our uniforms would end up the same colour—white—but we wouldn't smell.

"I'll do it now," I said.

"But you haven't finished your dinner," she called after me.

I had lost my appetite.

I was already in the hallway by the time I remembered that I didn't even have my gear. I grabbed my purse and was rummaging for the receipt with the phone number on it when the doorbell rang. Dark Eyes stood on the porch, my hockey bag in his hand.

"Hi," he said, a wide smile spread across his face.

"Uh, hi."

"I found your bag."

"Yeah, I see that. That's great. Thanks." I took it and tossed it into the hall behind me.

There was an awkward silence.

What? Was I supposed to tip him or something? I just wanted him off my front step before someone came along and saw him. But he just kept standing there.

Wait a minute.

"How did you know where I live?" I asked, crossing my arms.

"I know Will," he answered. "We gave him a ride home after a tournament once."

OK, so not a stalker. Still, it was time for him to leave.

"Well, thanks again," I said backing away.

"I was serious about my offer," he said.

Surely he wasn't referring to his 'I'll show you my moves' offer?

"I practise almost every day after school on the pond behind our place. Well, when it freezes over. You could come and, ah, work out?"

Lame. Lame. Lame. Did he think I was that naïve? I wasn't going anywhere near his practice pond so he could deliberately give me bad advice and have me make stupid plays on the ice. I could do that all by myself.

Besides, what if I just made a fool of myself, falling on my butt? An image of myself flailing helplessly flashed in my mind—but then, out of nowhere, so did an image of him catching me. And he was kinda cute...

Wait a minute! What was I thinking?

"Gee, thanks," I said, trying to shake off the imaginary feel of his arms around me. "Really. But I don't have time. Homework and stuff. You know. I get a lot. Of homework. But thanks. Really. Thanks."

I was babbling. Why was I babbling? The only other time I can remember babbling was when dreamy Greg Grant asked me for my phone number. He was two years older than me, with a deep mellow voice and dirty blond hair that kept falling in front of his eyes. You should have heard me babble when he asked for my phone number. I'm not sure there were any numbers in the mumbles that fell out of my mouth, but he scribbled something down and was gone. Turned out he called to ask my accountant dad a question about his tax return.

"Well, if you change your mind, or get less homework sometime, just come on over. It's the old stone house on the seventh concession. I'll be there." He was backing away from the door and almost fell off the step.

I clamped my lips shut to stop the smile starting to form. And to prevent any further babbling.

He gave a little wave and jumped off the step.

I shut the door.

OMG. I was attracted to a hockey player. Drat him and his soft dark eyes.

eight

Over the last month and a half we had played about half the teams in the league and were fourth in league standings. Pretty decent for a team with so many first-year players. Except for tonight. We were down five to nothing after only one period.

"I thought this team was supposed to be the worst in the league?" Rachel grumbled as she tried to catch her breath on the bench.

"According to the Tornadoes or Hurricanes or whatever weather system we played Tuesday, this team has a goalie like a sieve, can't pass the salt across the table let alone a puck across the ice, and has worse aim than a three-year-old boy in the bathroom," I said.

"They don't look like they are having any trouble with their aim tonight," Rachel said as they scored again.

"Are you sure we're playing the team they were referring to?" Lilly asked.

"They said the Greys," I said. "Which is *this* team—don't let the bright orange jerseys fool you. They said that the game was ours for the taking."

"Is that why Coach Santos put Diane in goal?" Lilly asked, wincing as Diane flopped from the left side of the net over to the right side.

"Yeah, he thought it was a good chance to give her some experience in net in case Sam ever has to miss a game," I said. Diane had looked horrified when he mentioned it. And with good reason. The other team was eating her alive. Pucks were flying at her from every direction. Sam was dying a thousand deaths on the bench, watching the carnage.

And what was with the referee? Every time we touched the puck, the whistle blew. I think he was making up penalties. I mean, "Playing with too many sticks"? All Andrea had done was try and give Lilly her stick back when it got knocked out of her hand. As she skated over with it, the ref blew his whistle and we got another penalty.

And worst of all, the Three Stooges were back. They were sitting a few rows up from the penalty box where, unfortunately, they had a lot of opportunities to make fun of us. We had served sixteen minutes of penalties already, but only played for twenty.

"What's up with Coach Santos?" Lilly asked me as we sat on the bench waiting for the second period to start. "I thought for sure he'd be frothing at the mouth over how we played the first period. He barely said a word."

"I know. No stomping, no swearing, no slamming his

palm on the wall behind the bench...maybe he's sick?"

The game had started up again and the puck was back in our end. Diane was in a panic. I couldn't watch.

"Why doesn't he pull her?" I asked Jenna beside me.

She leaned over. "I don't think he even remembers he put her in goal. Have you noticed how he keeps checking his phone? I'm telling you, something's going on."

As if on cue, Coach Santos pulled out his cell phone, checked the screen, and put it back in his pocket.

We looked back to the ice just as the ref's whistle blew. Another penalty. For us. This time it was against Andrea for falling on the puck. I kid you not.

Rachel, our captain, argued with the ref that it wasn't an intentional delay of game, that a player on the other team had actually tripped Andrea, and why wasn't he calling *that* penalty? I guess their conversation got a little heated because Rachel ended up sitting beside Andrea in the box. 'Unsportsmanlike conduct,' I think the ref called it.

I took the ice for another round of five on three. We did our best, really we did, but the Greys in their Creamsicle orange shirts were all over us. After thirty-three seconds, they scored. On the upside, at least we got Andrea back.

We had to wait at the blue line for a few minutes for the face-off while the refs sorted out something at the penalty box. I was lined up beside orange shirt number 6. She was snickering at something.

"What's your problem?" I grumbled to her.

"We heard you sucked, but your team brings suckage

to an all-time low," she sneered, loud enough for Rachel to hear her in the penalty box.

I turned around to look at Rachel and the colour of her face could only be described as maroon. She would have exploded if at that very moment the ref hadn't skated over for the face-off.

The puck dropped and we had to chase the other team into our end again. Four of us fought over the puck behind our net.

"Move, lard butt," Lilly said, shoving number 6 into the boards.

Number 6 shoved back and Lilly went sprawling onto the ice. She lay there, not moving.

I think the ref would have tried to ignore Lilly spread-eagled on the ice, but he was forced to blow the whistle before she became a speed bump.

I tried to help her up as the ref called a penalty on number 6.

That's when things really got nasty.

The other team thought Lilly was faking it and intentionally trying to draw a penalty.

"This isn't a league for wimps," number 6 yelled as the linesman led her to the penalty box. "Go back to your diamond and stay there!"

Weird. How did they know we were a softball team? It wasn't really a secret, but it wasn't exactly advertised, either.

Lilly glided back to the bench and sat down. She had the wind knocked out of her, but she was all right. Number 6 glared at her from the penalty box.

It was a different game on the ice now. Every chance they got, the other team jabbed us, poked us, and rammed us.

"You don't belong in this league, Roadrunner," I heard in my ear as I fought for the puck against the boards. "This is for serious hockey players."

I didn't say anything. What could I say? This had all started as a dare, after all.

Rachel was out of the box and beside me on the bench waiting for her turn back on the ice. Jenna was on the other side of her, rubbing her shoulder. "Dogface there got me with the end of her stick. You know, I've heard enough about how we don't belong here."

Jenna got the signal to go on the ice and hopped the boards, her jaw set and her eyes ablaze. She streaked after the puck. I watched in awe as she dodged a few enemy sticks, dug the puck out of the corner, and got a shot off on the goalie, but it was just wide and slid past the net.

I looked at Rachel and Andrea on either side of me. "Let's give Jenna some help out there."

Rachel was up in a flash. "I'm ready to kick butt."

"They want game?" Andrea said, going over the boards. "We'll give them game."

It was time we showed them that we *were* serious... maybe not so much about the sport, but definitely serious about *this* game. And when we pulled together as a team, we were a force to be reckoned with.

The renewed determination in the three of us spread through our team like a virus. We did everything we could to get control of the puck and then we hung on to it. We were starting to get some shots on goal.

The whistle blew. Another penalty for the enemy. Someone got caught butt-ending with their stick.

"I think we're unnerving them. They're angry and that's making them make mistakes," Rachel said, huffing and puffing on the bench.

I think she was right. Jenna's line scrambled for the puck in front of the enemy's net and Grace managed to sneak it in under the goalie's pads for our first goal.

"Well, at least they won't have skunked us," I said.

"Two minutes, fifteen seconds left in the period," Rachel said, looking at me and winking. "Time enough for another goal before the break. I'm going to put this one in."

And she did. Like I said: pitbull.

I looked over at Coach Santos after Rachel scored, but he was in the hallway to the dressing room, his back to the game, talking on his cell phone. He moved out of the way as we squeezed by for the break, but kept on talking.

We sat in the dressing room waiting for Coach Santos to come in and ream us out. What would it be? How disappointed he was in us? What terrible players we were? Maybe a two-hour practice starting at 4 am?

But he never came in. We finished our drinks, re-laced our skates and went back out to the bench. Our coach had disappeared.

nine

"So, is it even legal to play without your coach?" Andrea asked.

"I think technically he's supposed to be here before we take the ice," I said.

"So what do we do now?" Jenna asked.

Rachel snorted. "Do? We go out and wipe the Greys' butts all over the ice."

"I mean about Coach Santos?" Andrea said.

Everyone on the bench was looking around trying to spot him. He was nowhere to be seen.

"Has this ever happened before?" I asked Kayla. She'd been on the team for a couple of years now.

She shook her head.

"Looks like we're in charge then," Rachel said. "And as captain I am making the executive decision to put Sam back in goal."

"'Bout time," Sam grumbled, shoving her helmet

down on her head and skating to the net. Diane looked as though she was going to faint with relief.

"Do you think the refs will let us play without our coach?"

"They'd better. I'm not giving those orange Grey dweebs the satisfaction of forfeiting the game. We're staying and finishing this." Rachel's expression said she was going to enjoy it, too.

The referee skated over. "Where's your coach?"

"Oh, he had a small emergency. He'll be back soon," Rachel said smoothly.

The referee looked skeptical. We looked innocent. The referee spoke to the linesman and then blew the whistle to start the third period.

My line was first up. Was it a coincidence that I was paired up with number 6 at the edge of the circle again? I think not.

"Your coach had the right idea," number 6 said.

"What?"

"You should all just slink away back to your parks to play tag with your spongy ball."

She didn't just say 'slink away' to me, did she? We don't slink anywhere; certainly not from a game we've started. And spongy ball? There is *nothing* spongy about a softball. She'd obviously never been beaned in the face with one going 50 miles an hour. Ask Zoe Watson who stopped playing after having her nose broken by a wild pitch.

The puck dropped. Ten players fought over that little rubber disk like it was the last brownie in the pan.

Back and forth down the ice we careened, each team trying to get control of the puck and keep it.

Andrea tried to get it out of our end and flicked it up in the air. Number 17 from the other team caught it in her glove and dropped it on the ice. She tried to pass it to her teammate down the ice but I intercepted the pass and took off with the puck. I could hear the Three Stooges yelling at me to pour it on.

Rachel and Andrea positioned themselves in front and to the right of the net. I passed to Rachel who deflected it straight to Andrea. Andrea pulled back and let fly.

Goal!

Six to three. Oh yeah.

There was no time to celebrate, though. The other team quickly answered with a goal of their own. But we weren't done yet. A beautiful play on Jenna's line helped Lilly find the back of the net.

"Biscuit, meet basket," she said, getting high fives from the bench.

I managed to poke the puck under the goalie's pads in a scramble in front of the net and Rachel got it over the line again with only three minutes left. The game ended seven to five.

Not bad.

We got up to leave. The Three Stooges had made their way around the arena to the seats that lined the hall to our dressing room.

"Now if you gals had just played that way in the first period, you could've put them away," Tyler said.

I looked up into the seats. My eyes locked with Kip's. He smiled. I ducked my head quickly.

"And if you clowns spent more time training and less time bothering us, you would be standing better than third in your own league," Andrea said.

"Hey! Our prodigies are following our games!" Braydon crowed.

Andrea threw her glove at him.

"So are you gonna come cheer us on at our game tomorrow against the Eagles?"

"Sorry," Andrea said, with a small toss of her head, "but we've got a group manicure planned for tomorrow." The other girls laughed. Our fingers spend their time inside of smelly gloves and picking balls off the dusty ground; we keep our nails plain and short.

Braydon looked genuinely disappointed. "We could really use your support. We haven't beaten the Eagles all year."

"It's going to be a great game," Kip said.

"We'll see," Andrea said, shrugging. The girls moved down the hall to the dressing room.

Sam, Rachel, and I were last off the bench but were stopped in our tracks by a voice calling from the other bench, "Hey, it was nice to beat you Roadrunners. Let's do it again sometime, OK?"

The three of us exchanged looks. Oh, we wanted to do it again, all right. Only the next time the outcome was going to be different.

We hurried to the dressing room to get the scoop on Coach Santos. I was sure he'd be there explaining where he was and why he had abandoned us in the third period.

"He had better have a good excuse for ditching us," Andrea said when we found that the dressing room was empty.

"Yeah, he could have at least texted one of us," Sam said. "I mean, how much energy does it take to move your thumbs?"

"Unless he was incapacitated in a full body cast or something," Lilly said.

"We can only hope," Rachel said.

"Whatever it is, he'll probably explain himself tomorrow at practice," I said, "and everything will be back to normal."

Boy, was I ever wrong.

ten

It was hard to drag myself out of bed the next morning. Something had to be done about these 5 am practices. It was cruel and unusual punishment.

We were all still pretty annoyed with Coach Santos's disappearing act yesterday.

"As far as I'm concerned," Sam said, "he could have been admitted to Emerg with an allergic reaction so bad he looks like Quasimodo and it still doesn't excuse him for ditching us at our game yesterday."

She had a point. He could have at least told one of us that he had to leave. And now he was late showing up for practice, too.

"Well, I'm not waiting any longer," Rachel said. "I'm going to warm up."

We followed her onto the ice. No one really wanted to be left in the dressing room to inhale the wrath of Santos when he did finally come and comment on our game yesterday.

After skating around the rink to warm our muscles up, we decided to skate the circles on the ice. Pucks would have been great to work with, but until Mr. Santos arrived with the equipment bag, we were on our own, puckless.

"So, are you really going to the Hornets' game tonight, Andrea?" Sam asked.

"I think so," she answered.

"Why?" Rachel, Sam, and I asked in unison. Hadn't those guys tormented us enough?

"Well, I know the Three Stooges have been a bit of a pain, but Tyler overheard me in the halls talking to Jenna about that fumbled pass I made last game and he gave me a good stickhandling tip. And besides, my cousins live in Julian Falls and I happen to know some of the players on the Eagles' team. They are a bunch of smug apes and I'd love to see them taken down by the Hornets." She paused and looked at us. "Anyone want to come with me? Or are you all going to leave me there looking like a hockey groupie?"

Now how could we not agree to join her when she put it like that?

It was twenty minutes into our practice and we were getting bored. Out of desperation we started playing 'red light, green light' to practice quick starts and stops. I hadn't played that game in years but I had it in the bag when I noticed Coach Santos standing by the bench. He waved us over.

We gathered around him.

Coach cleared his throat a couple of times before saying, "I'm not going to be coaching you anymore."

He let that hang in the air for a minute. "Sorry to leave you mid-season, but I've been asking around for someone to replace me." He ran a hand through his thinning hair. "You've put out a good effort but I gotta tell you, it isn't easy to find someone around here willing to take on a girls' team. I was thinking maybe one of your parents would step up?"

Silence.

"You're dumping us?" Sam sputtered, "and you want us to ask our parents to coach us like some Mini Mites beginners' team?"

Mr. Santos' face reddened slightly. "No. Not dumping. Um, just moving forward in my career. I've had another coaching offer and I feel that I need to prioritize my life. My coaching skills would be better utilized by a team that was, ah, more experienced."

I was speechless. The red was creeping up Rachel's neck.

"So, I wish you all luck and I'll keep my eyes open for someone to fill my shoes."

He turned and was gone.

There was silence on the ice as we all absorbed that little speech.

Sam was the first to speak. "Someone willing to take on a girls' team? We're fourth in league standings! Out of ten teams!" Sam threw her gloves on the ice.

"A good effort, my butt! We were out there giving it our all and he was either screaming at us or talking on the phone!" Andrea added.

"Well, at least now we know what those 'suits' were

doing here at our other game," Jenna said. "They were obviously scoping out how he was doing, and while we were busting our chops on the ice, we were making him look good. Good enough to get a coaching job with another team!"

"A boys' team," Lilly said. "Probably triple-A, too."

She was right, of course. We were the only girls' team around, after all. He had used us to get a better job and then tossed us aside. Never mind the fact that we had made the commitment to play for the whole season; he had obviously only committed himself until something better came along.

I should have been relieved. I mean, wasn't this the perfect solution? No one could accuse us of giving up on a sport we hadn't really wanted to play in the first place. It was our coach who had left. So why did I feel so let down?

We trudged off the ice to the dressing room.

"I guess things will go back to normal now," Andrea said. She got a few mumbled agreements.

"I gotta tell you, though," Lilly said. "I sure would have loved to have taken another crack at the Greys."

I threw my gloves in my hockey bag and realized—so would I.

eleven

I was surprised how many people had turned out for the Hornets' midget hockey game. We were lucky if there were three or four mothers at our games. Entire families had come out to this. The kids were running around the upper level while the adults hugged coffee cups to keep their hands warm.

In the end, most of our team had shown up at the game. We decided it would be a fitting farewell to our short but intense hockey careers.

Judging by the way the guys delighted in shooting pucks at the glass in front of us to make us jump during warm up, they seemed pleased to see us.

I had a new appreciation for the game now that I had played it myself. It sure is easy to sit in the stands and yell when you're not the one going flat out and trying to control the puck, too.

Braydon crouched at centre ice for the face-off. The puck dropped and the battle began. Already there was pushing and shoving. It was going to be a wild game.

The boards rattled with the force of a hard check. Kip was pinned by a tank of a hockey player. Really, did anyone verify these guys' birth certificates? There was no way he was in the same age range as the Hornets. Not unless he had been fed concrete as a toddler. Kip was able to wriggle free and take off. Not only was he cute, but he could move, too. I got to thinking that maybe I should have let him show me his moves when I had the chance.

The Hornets were matching the Eagles play for play. It was intense. Twelve minutes into the period, the Hornets had the puck and were charging down the ice, three on two. It took me a second to realize it was Tyler, Braydon, and Kip. Braydon made a drop pass to Tyler, but instead of shooting, Tyler passed it to Kip, who flicked it up over the left shoulder of the Eagle goalie. *Score!* I had to admit, it was a sweet goal.

We were on our feet cheering. The guys skated past their bench for a row of high fives. Kip looked over to where we were sitting and smiled. My stomach did that flip-flop thing again.

"Did you see the way Tyler passed the puck without even looking? It's like they know where their teammates are going to be before they get there," Lilly's mouth was hanging open in admiration. "Like they're psychic or something."

"Psychic hockey?" Rachel said. "Now that would be a cool sport."

"Do you think if we practised enough we could be psychic players, too?" I asked, wondering how long it would take to be as tuned in for hockey as we were for softball.

"Without a coach we're never going to find out," Rachel said.

"Oh, right," I said, feeling stupid. How could I forget the team dumping of this morning? It was strange. I thought I would be happier than this. But...it felt like we were just on the brink of really getting the hang of the game.

The second period started with a penalty for the Hornets. Too many men on the ice. You could see the whole team cringe at such a dumb mistake. One thing you did *not* want was to be a man down against a team like the Eagles.

The Hornets' goalie couldn't really be blamed for the goal that came fifty seconds later. The Eagles were relentless on the powerplay.

Back at full strength, the Hornets turned it on. Back and forth across the rink, the battle raged. With only a minute left in the period, a sloppy pass on the Hornets' side gave the Eagles the chance they needed. They tore down the rink and put it in the Hornets' net before they could even react. Two to one. It was a bad way to end the second period.

"Hey, isn't that Santos leaning on the railing up there?" Sam asked, squinting up into the stands.

"It is," Rachel said, her eyes narrowing.

Right then Mr. Santos looked our way and I saw Rachel start to lift her hand as if she was going to make an obscene gesture. I grabbed her hand and pulled it back down, not wanting to tick him off before he found us a replacement. He turned his back to us and kept talking to the man beside him.

"Did you see that?" Rachel asked. "He didn't even acknowledge our existence."

"Saxitoxin is too kind a death for him. It's quick. No suffering," Lilly said vehemently.

I had to agree. That was just plain nasty of him to ignore us. A girls' team was good enough when he didn't have another gig, and now he pretended not to see us?

"It's the perfect murder weapon," Rachel said.

"Yes, except it's too hard to come by. I don't know how my heroine would get some." Lilly looked pensive. "I think I'll have to resort to a good old-fashioned stabbing."

"But you'd have a problem getting rid of the murder weapon," Rachel said, still pulling for saxitoxin.

"Unless it was an icicle," I said, wondering if Lilly would acknowledge me in her book if I came up with a cool idea. "Then it would just melt away."

You could see the gears turning in Lilly's mind. "An icicle? Hmmmm. That's brilliant!" She gave me a big hug.

The guys came out for the last period. Both teams skated around to show how unconcerned they were about the score. As if. The Eagles looked arrogant and the Hornets looked determined. The puck dropped. Minutes ticked by as we were on the edge of our seats willing the guys to score, but it wasn't happening.

The whistle blew for a slashing call against the Hornets. Braydon, as captain, argued with the referee but it did no good. Number 3 skated to the penalty box and slammed the door. Oh, boy. I knew how that felt.

The guys were going to have to be amazing on defence to keep the Eagles from scoring with a man advantage.

Kip and Braydon were out to hold down the fort. The Eagles easily got the puck and set up in the Hornets' end. They passed back and forth waiting for the perfect moment to fire on the goalie. The four Hornets did their best to cover all angles. One Eagle positioned back by the blue line pretended to shoot, but at the last second decided to pass to his teammate on the other side. His hesitation was enough for Kip. He lunged forward, stole the puck, and took off for the Eagles' end.

I was so tense my muscles felt like steel cables. Kip skated straight at the goalie; faked left, faked right, and then put it right up over his right shoulder. A short-handed goal! Now *that* was awesome.

We jumped out of our seats, cheering. Kip got his congratulatory smacks on the shoulders and head from his teammates and then flashed me a dazzling smile. Well, I thought it was dazzling. Then again, maybe it was just his white mouth guard.

The game was tied with seven minutes left. I didn't know how I would stand any more of this suspense. It would have been easier to be on the ice than in the seats watching. At least on the ice you have some control over the outcome of the game. Up in the stands, all we could do was watch.

Both teams took their spots for the face-off. There was a scramble for the puck. The Eagles got control of the puck, the Hornets stole it back. Back and forth it went, with the boards rattling and blades cutting on ice. A weak pass gave the Eagles a shot on our net. The Hornets' goalie saw it coming, stopped it with his pads, and fell on it just to be sure. The whistle blew.

I wheezed. I didn't realize I had been holding my breath. Kip's line was back on and there was just over two minutes left.

The clock ticked down; one minute left. It was now or never. Braydon got the puck, passed it to Kip, who passed it to Tyler. The clock was running down in seconds now. The puck went back to Kip, to Braydon, and when I thought that the buzzer was going to sound at any time, a nice little flick of the wrist put it in the net.

Just 1.9 seconds left on the clock! We were on our feet, screaming and stomping. What a game!

We watched the Hornets congratulate each other on the ice as we gathered up our stuff.

"Hey," Andrea called to the rest of us over the noise. "It would serve Santos right if we somehow managed to snag another coach ourselves and make it to the finals."

"And we could do it, too," Rachel said. "We were on the brink of greatness."

Now, I think the 'brink of greatness' was a going a little too far, but Rachel always did think big.

"Do you think we could?" I asked. "Find a new coach, I mean? I was kinda enjoying our winter training."

"I'm sure we could," Rachel said. "Let's get the rest of the team to meet us at the Burger Bar in half an hour for a team meeting."

We left the arena with a renewed hope. The Roadrunners weren't going away without a fight.

twelve

"So, where exactly do we find a new coach?" Sam asked, raising her voice to be heard over the après-game crowd in the Burger Bar. "It would be too much to ask for it to be as easy as some Internet site with 'coaches for hire' or something, right?"

"What we need is a Coaches Depot, so we could pick out a decent one this time. Someone who doesn't spend the whole time watching everything BUT the game while trying to advance his career," Andrea said.

"I want to go to a Coaches R Us so we can go up and down the aisles and try them out. You know, see how abrasive their voices are, how well they know the rules, how they look in a suit," Rachel added.

"Rachel!" Lilly said, and laughed. No one had to bother mentioning that Mr. Santos was definitely NOT Ryan Reynolds in a suit.

"Well, until someone finds a Coaches Depot or

Coaches R Us, we're going to have to do this the old-fashioned way: networking," I said. "So, what are our options? Or I guess I should say, who are our options?"

"We could ask my neighbour, Mr. Mitchell," Deb said. "I think he used to coach hockey."

"Isn't he a bit old for coaching?" Andrea asked. "Besides, I don't think he'd make it across the ice to the bench with his walker." She thought for a moment. "How about Matt Landry? I heard he just came back from Junior A."

"You mean got *kicked out* of Junior A," Rachel said. "Would you really like to be on the receiving end of THAT temper if we had a bad game?" She shuddered. "How about that cute guy who works in the All Sports All The Time store? Now *he'd* look great in a suit!"

"Oh, he's wearing a suit all right," Jenna said, grinning. "Only it's an orange one with a number stencilled on it. He's doing a two-year stretch for embezzling from the store."

"He's in jail?" I asked, stunned. He had worked wonders finding me a decent softball glove that still fit my tiny hand. "Bummer."

The table grew silent.

"For crying out loud, guys, there's got to be someone in a town this size who will coach us," I said.

"Maybe I know someone," Lilly said. "My dad's cousin is huge into hockey and coached a few years ago."

"Do you think he'd be willing to coach us?" I asked.

"She," Lilly said.

"A woman coach?" Andrea's eyebrows shot up. "I've

never had a woman coach for anything before. Is she any good?"

"She took her teams to the championships twice."

"OK, team vote. Who's in favour of calling up..." Rachel hesitated, "What's her name?"

"Sister Helen."

"I thought she was your dad's cousin?" Kayla interrupted.

"She's not *my* sister, she's *a* sister," Lilly said.

"A sister?" Rachel asked. "Like a nun?"

"Yeah, like a nun."

"A nun? Are you kidding me? Are they even allowed to be coaches?" Rachel sputtered.

Andrea groaned. "If you thought we were teased before, can you imagine what would happen if people saw our coach in a penguin suit?"

Lilly sighed. "She's a modern nun. She doesn't wear a habit. And yes, it's allowed."

"I don't know, Lilly. Thanks for the idea, but it seems a bit, ah, radical," I said.

There was a shuffle of bodies in the seats behind me. I instantly regretted turning around to see a booth full of Hornets nudging each other and smirking. Well, all smirking except for Kip. He was smiling and staring straight at me. I hoped I wasn't blushing.

"Look, guys! Our fan club is here!" Tyler crowed to his teammates who were grinning like idiots. "So, ladies? How'd you enjoy the game?"

They deserved to be taunted and ridiculed like they had done to us, but you know what? I couldn't do it.

I shrugged and said, "Could've gone either way in the end."

"Are you kidding?" Tyler said. "We had that in the bag from the get-go."

"Your goalie saved your butt with that snag in the third period," Sam said, defending goalies everywhere.

"That's still only a tie unless we put it in the net. And we did," Braydon said, lifting his chin slightly.

"You know," Tyler said, putting an arm on the top of the bench between the booths, "it's too bad about your team or we could have set up some guys versus the girls matches and really shown you how it's done."

The red started creeping up Rachel's neck. "What do you mean, 'about our team'?" she asked.

"We heard about Santos," Braydon said. "Word is that he stuck it out with the Roadrunners just to make a point to the brass."

"What point?" I asked.

"You know. If he was able to turn girls into hockey players, then they would realize how valuable he was and give him another team."

"You're making that up," I said.

"That's the word," Tyler said. "And it looks like it worked. And, you know, with you gals not having a coach it looks like we won the bet..."

"It wasn't a bet, it was a dare. And you haven't won anything. As it happens, we already have a new coach," Rachel blurted.

What was Rachel saying? We didn't have a coach. We didn't even have any prospects except for a senior citizen, an anger-management flunkie, a convicted felon, and a nun.

"Oh, ho!" Braydon said. "A new coach? Who is he?"

"Who is *she*," Rachel said.

Oh lord. The nun.

"A woman coach?" Braydon erupted into laughter. "Oh, you are making this too easy. If a tough guy like Santos couldn't whip you into shape, no woman can."

"Who says we weren't already in shape?" I said. "Fourth in our league is nothing to hang our heads about." Their arrogance was starting to get on my nerves. It's not like the Hornets had never had a bad year. Granted, most years they made it easily to the playoffs, but I remember once when they choked in an important game and got knocked out in the first round.

"Yeah, and what rock did you crawl out from under?" Rachel added. "There are women coaches at every level of hockey, right up to the national Olympic team, even if we've never had one here because we happen to live in a hick town with caveman attitudes. Our new coach is used to taking teams to the championships, and we'll be no different."

I didn't like where this was going.

"The championships?" Braydon looked to his teammates as if to make sure they had all heard the same thing. "You're saying that not only will you last the whole season, but you'll make the finals?"

"You don't have to make it sound like it's a crazy idea, Braydon," Rachel said. "We're a good team that hasn't even hit its stride. Even if we don't make the finals, we've got more going for us than the Hornets do, judging from today's performance."

Braydon left the booth and came around to our table. He held out his hand to Rachel. "Wanna make it official? A bet this time, not a dare."

"What bet?"

"The team with the higher standing at the end of regular season play in their league wins. A tie will go to the ladies." He bowed like he was doing us a favour.

Rachel stood up.

"What are the stakes?" she asked.

Braydon looked over at his table and smiled. "The losing team has to be the cheerleading squad for the winning team all next season."

Oh, the implications of that were obvious. They thought they were going to win and we'd have to spend next year in skimpy outfits with our parts bouncing up and down as we cheered. This was dangerous.

"Rachel, ignore them," I said in what I hoped was a soothing voice. "The guys are just being jerks. We don't have to prove anything to them. They're just mad that they were wrong about us."

I pulled her back down onto the bench.

Now Tyler walked over. "Wrong about you? You're a bunch of girls used to playing *softball*—that's not even real baseball! It's bad enough that a decent coach like Santos dumped you. Now you're going to have a woman teach you hockey?"

"Santos—a decent coach?" I said, unable to believe I had heard right. "Are you blind? You guys were at some of our games. Did you ever see him pay attention to us or what was going on on the ice?" I was on my feet now, my voice getting shriller with every word. "He was so busy talking on his cell and staring at the suits up on the rail that he didn't even know who was in net."

Tyler was right up in my face. "He was a great coach for the midget team. You don't want to take the bet because you know we're right."

"You're on," I said, grabbing Braydon's hand and shaking it. "And just for the record, we expect you to have pompoms in our team colours."

I stormed out of the Burger Bar practically hyperventilating. Did I really just do that? Alone, out in the fresh air, I put my face in my hands. What a stupid, stupid thing to do. Rachel was usually the headstrong and impulsive one.

The door of the Burger Bar opened and I took a deep cleansing breath. I looked up to see my team staring at me.

"Now, look here, Tara," Rachel said, standing in front of me with her hands on her hips. "Flying off the handle and agreeing to stupid bets is *my* specialty."

She broke into a grin. "But I have to say, the pompom thing was a nice touch."

At this everyone laughed.

"I'll go back in and get us out of this," I said, relieved they weren't furious with me.

"Get us out of this? No way!" Andrea said. "If you or Rachel hadn't taken the bet, I would have!"

There were nods all around.

"These guys need to be taught a lesson," Andrea continued. "I'm tired of us girls getting a pat on the head and sent to the back of the line. Do we get any recognition for our placing in the softball finals? Our Provincial win two years ago? Our Midwestern Conference Tournament gold medals?"

"Not to mention our kick-ass fourth place standing in a tough league in our first season of hockey," Sam added.

"But what if we don't win?" I asked. "I don't think I could stand being the Hornets' cheerleaders for a whole year."

Rachel made a *pfft* sound. "It's not like it would be any different from how the town thinks of us already: pretty girls instead of athletes. But if we win, this could be our chance to show the men that we have skills, too."

"And drive," Sam said.

"And commitment," Jenna added.

"And don't let those hyenas in there kid you," Rachel went on. "The Hornets are struggling this year. My dad said they'll be lucky to make it to the finals."

"Well, then," I said, relief washing over me, "let's make sure *we* make it to the finals."

We high fived each other.

"Of course, that leaves just one little problem," I said.

"Getting a coach," Andrea said. "I guess it's time to call the nun."

thirteen

"So what did she say?" I asked Lilly at our table in the cafeteria.

"Well, she has some scheduling conflicts, but Sister Helen's on board," Lilly said. "She said she'll work things out and meet us at the arena for our next practice."

We breathed a sigh of relief.

"This is great," I gushed. "The way the schedule worked out, we only had to cancel one game against the Turkey Vultures..."

"Goldenhawks," Rachel sighed.

"...whatever, some bird team, which we can reschedule. And the last time I checked we were still sitting fourth in the standings."

"The Hornets are second," Jenna said.

"Yeah, but they lost their game last night," Sam said, "and we're just getting going."

I hoped we were going in the right direction.

"So where does a nun learn to play hockey?" I asked Lilly.

"My dad used to play shinny with her three brothers," Lilly said. "She was always bugging them to join their game. Finally, they thought they could get rid of her by saying she could play, but only if she scored a goal in the first ten minutes."

"Well," Rachel asked, "did she?"

"Nope," Lilly answered. "She scored two. After that, they fought over who got to have her on their team. Dad said she was something else on the ice. She kept playing when she went to university, but then stopped when she joined the order."

"Was she not allowed to play anymore?" Rachel asked.

Lilly shook her head. "No. She wrecked her knee. So she started coaching."

"If she's so good," Sam asked, "why isn't she coaching another team?"

"She just got back from doing some sort of mission work in Africa. She hadn't really looked into it for this season."

I went back to my chicken wrap while I thought about a hockey-playing nun. I tried to imagine her in skates putting us through some drills at our practice tomorrow morning. It was no use. All I could picture was Maria von Trapp from "The Sound of Music" teaching us to yodel.

The dressing room was pretty quiet. There were no rude

jokes, no throwing of undergarments, no swearing. It was actually kinda funny how just the thought of a nun coming in put us on our best behaviour.

When the door opened, I swear I was holding my breath.

What a disappointment. In walked an ordinary-looking woman in blue pants and a beige sweater. The only thing the least bit nunnish about her was a little gold cross pinned to her sweater.

"Hi everyone," she said. "Lilly told me you were looking for a new coach." She looked around. No one moved.

"You *are* looking for a new coach, yes?"

We had all become deaf mutes.

Lilly finally spoke up. "Hi, Sister Helen! Yes, we are desperate for a coach."

"Oh, good," Sister Helen said, "because for a minute there, I thought I was in the wrong arena." She smiled.

I tried to smile back but it felt like my face was frozen.

Sister Helen sighed. "Is it the nun thing?" She looked around at us. "Well, why don't we get that out of the way right now. Let's see. FAQs: Yes, I am a real nun. No, our order does not require us to wear a habit. Yes, I like being a nun and have been one for twelve years. No, obviously I did not take a vow of silence. Yes, I did take vows of chastity and poverty, but no, that does not mean I have to be a hermit or live in a cardboard box and starve. Did I miss anything?"

"Where *do* you live?" Andrea asked.

"I share an apartment with two other sisters."

"What do you do, you know, as your job? Do you just

sit around and pray and stuff?" Sam asked, blushing a little.

Sister Helen stifled a smile. "I work at the youth crisis centre three days a week, and work with our parish to set up programs for at-risk youth the rest of the time. But," now she was smiling, "I do pray and stuff, too. Any more questions?"

"Do you get in trouble if you do something wrong or swear or whatever?" Jenna asked.

"No." She laughed a nice soft laugh. "I don't get in trouble, but I'm supposed to be setting a good example for others, so I try to watch my behaviour. But believe me when I say there will never be a 'Saint Helen Turcott.' OK? Are we good?"

This time there were genuine smiles around the room.

"If you have any other questions, just ask. Oh, and you can just call me Helen or Coach. But right now, let's get down to hockey. Lilly tells me that you are sitting about fourth in your league. I'll be mostly watching you today to get a feel for your team's strengths and weaknesses. So, everyone on the ice to warm up."

It felt good to get moving but if we thought she was going to go easy on us, we were wrong. We did drills for passing, puck control, shooting, stick-handling and skating. We thought Coach Santos was tough...Coach Helen was tougher. There wasn't one bad pass or sloppy shot that she didn't catch. By the end of it we were soaked with sweat.

"All right, ladies. I'll take my notes here and work out a practice routine for us," Coach Helen said. "For now,

I guess I'll see you at the game, Friday night...." She squinted at the page in front of her, "...at 11:30 pm? Is that right?"

I nodded. "We don't have the best ice times."

"We'll have to see about that," she said, more to herself than to us, I think.

fourteen

I shouldn't have been surprised to bump into Sam at Hannah's Bakery. Saturday mornings were prime time at the bakery with practically the entire town in line waiting patiently for a caffeine and sugar fix. Most looked like they had just crawled out of bed and hadn't even changed out of their pajama pants. I fit right in with an impressive bed head, all matted and tangled. I hadn't bothered to tame it for the bakery line-up...we all looked pretty much the same.

"Do you think a half dozen donuts will help me forget last night's game?" Sam asked, slipping in behind me.

"No, I think you need a full dozen," I said, meaning it. "That game was the stinker to end all stinkers." I shook my head in disgust thinking about the beating we had taken from the Stingrays the night before.

I stepped up to the counter. "An apple turnover, two

fudge brownies, and a large hot chocolate, Dolores," I said.

"Here, I think you need a lemon tart, too," Dolores said, putting my pastries in a bag.

"You heard about the game, huh?" I asked.

"Oh, yeah. And what's this about a bet?"

"You heard about that, too?" Sam asked from behind.

Dolores nodded. "The guys were in here crowing about your loss and the bet and how hot you girls were gonna look in black spandex. What's that all about?"

I cringed, knowing that two of the goals against us last night were directly my fault. I had missed an easy pass and coughed up the puck, which gave the other team a breakaway. And worse than that, I accidentally knocked the puck into our own goal in a scramble in front of the net. I had wanted to crawl under the bench and stay there. What a first impression to make for our new coach.

"They bet us that they'll have a higher standing in their league at the end of the season than we will," I said, moving out of the way so Sam could get her dozen donuts.

"And the price?" Dolores asked.

I couldn't help wincing as I said, "The losers have to be the cheerleading squad for the winners all next season."

Dolores' eyes opened wide. "Ah, the black spandex. I think you girls better get some extra practice time in. Next!"

Sam and I pushed our way out of the store and braced ourselves against the wind.

"I guess all we can hope is that the Hornets keep dropping in the standings now that Kip Russell is out for a while," Sam said.

"Out? What happened?"

"Concussion. He took a nasty check in the last game and went head first into the boards."

"Wow, I hope he's OK."

"I heard that the doctor wants him out until Christmas. So, I guess I'll see you Monday morning at practice," Sam said, turning for home.

I wondered if Coach Helen would bother to show up for the practice or whether she would dump us after last night. I was deep in thought, hoping there was some nun rule about having to stick with hopeless cases or something, when I ran smack into someone, spilling my hot chocolate all over their jacket. A Hornets jacket, no less.

"Whoa!" the jacket said.

It was Kip. Perfect. I looked a mess. My eyes were puffy, I was wearing my brother's hoodie with the rip in the sleeve, and I couldn't remember if I had brushed my teeth or not.

"Geez, I'm sorry," I said, trying to hold my half-full cup of the hot chocolate and my bag of goodies in the same hand so I could try and smooth down my troll hair with the other. "Have I ruined it?"

He was smiling. "It's washable," he said, shaking the worst of it off. His mouth twitched as he looked at my hair.

"What?" I snarked. Why, oh, why couldn't I have at

least introduced my hair to a brush before leaving the house?

"I just wanted to say...ah..." He tried to avert his eyes from my head. "That was a rough game last night."

"You were there?" I groaned quietly. Was there any chance he had gone to the snack counter for something to eat just before I put the puck in my own net?

"Tough break with that last goal."

Nope. He saw it. I braced myself.

"You know, I did that once."

Hold on.

"You did?" I'm sure my mouth hanging open did nothing to help my appearance.

Kip nodded. "It was a playoff game, too. Luckily the rest of the team made up for my epic mistake and we still won."

"Yeah, but that wasn't my only goof-up." What was it about Kip that made me want to confess? "I couldn't take a pass if my life depended on it. It was like the puck was possessed or something."

"Your team should have been there to step up and support you if you were having a bad night. That goal was their mistake as much as yours."

Uh, was he being nice to me?

"You were pretty tense the whole game." He bent down to show me what he meant. "You had no give with your arms when you got the puck. You were so uptight that you held the stick like it was a concrete post." He straightened up again. "Look, why don't you come by my place after lunch. I'm gonna be on the pond practising and we could try some passes."

Wait. A. Minute.

"So, you're gonna help me out so you can lose the bet? As if."

"It's not like helping you with your passing is going to change anything—we're still going to win," he said with a smile. "Besides, the bet is stupid."

"Really? Then why didn't you say anything at the Burger Bar? You were right there. You could have spoken up at any time." I folded my arms as best I could while juggling my cup and bag.

"Who had a chance to say anything? You jumped up and shook Braydon's hand to seal the deal pretty fast."

I felt my face growing hot. "You still could have said you thought it was stupid," I countered.

Kip started to look uncomfortable. "It's not like they would've listened to me, anyway. I'm not too good when it comes to, you know, confrontations."

Sounded like a cop-out to me. It was time I told him I wasn't that naïve. It was time I said that I wasn't going to fall for his dark-eyed, smooth-talking tricks.

"Is one o'clock too early?" came out of my mouth. If I had had a hand free, I would have smacked my forehead.

Kip smiled. "One's fine."

Weak. That's what I was. Weak for dark-eyed smooth talkers.

Ten minutes to one found me at the end of the lane that

led to the pond. Kip had given me directions and I was a little surprised by his house. Somehow I had pictured a big mansion-type place in a fancy subdivision, not a century stone house nestled in a group of massive pine trees on the outskirts of town.

I biked down the lane, grateful that the freezing temperatures over the last few weeks had only brought a dusting of snow so I could still bike. Kip was already there, skating back and forth shooting at the net. He waved when he saw me.

"Wanna do a few laps as a warm up?" he asked as I laced my skates.

"Sure, but I was thinking—are you even allowed to be on the ice? I heard you got hurt at the last game and had to sit out a few."

"It's just a mild concussion, but because it's my second one, the doc is being extra careful. I can practise as long as I don't have any headaches or anything—and I have to avoid having my bell rung for a while."

Relieved, I stepped onto the ice and smiled. It was pretty smooth for a pond with only the odd bump. Along the edges a few dead stems poked through the ice.

Kip skated up alongside me and matched me stride for stride. The silence was a bit awkward so I searched for something to say.

"You come here often?" No, seriously. Did I just use a pick-up line?

Kip started laughing.

"I mean, do you practise out here a lot?" I hoped the cold wind was keeping my face from turning red.

"Yeah," he said, wearing the most adorable grin. "I do. I like working on drills when I'm alone so no one can see when I mess up. So, let's work on your passing."

"We did lots of passing drills with Santos, but I'm still not very good at it," I said.

"He might have done a lot of drills, but if he didn't correct your hands and feet, then it was a waste of time."

Kip turned out to be a good teacher. We started by just passing the puck back and forth, standing still. Then we moved on to passing while we were both moving, then passing while one of us was standing still and the other was moving.

I was doing pretty well except I wasn't rolling my wrists. I have no idea why wrists need to be rolled when you receive a puck, but apparently it was important enough for Kip to have to show me. Did I object to his standing behind me and reaching around with his strong masculine arms? No, indeed. In fact, I became so bad at wrist rolling that he had to show me several times.

"Had enough?" he asked, when I started to shiver.

"I think so." I sat on the makeshift wooden bench to take my skates off. "So, really now—why are you helping me? Aren't you going to get in trouble for aiding the enemy?"

"First, you're not the enemy. You girls really show some promise and were just unlucky enough to get stuck with Santos."

I looked up, shocked. Kip was the first person outside of our own team to say something negative about Mr. Santos. "We didn't have much choice; it was the only girls' team around with spots on the roster. We thought we were lucky they needed players...now I think I know why."

Kip began unlacing his skates, too. "I think it was a good thing you lost him when you did, before he did too much damage. I've heard good things about your new coach. Word is, she was a first-rate player and now makes a first-rate coach."

"Uh, you know she's a nun, right?"

Kip looked sideways at me, grinning. "Well, as long as she is there to coach you and not just convert you, I don't see it matters."

"Well, thanks again for this," I said, then added shyly, "Do you really think we show promise?"

"Yeah. Actually I think with a little more practice, you girls could give any team in your league a run for their money."

"I still don't get why you're helping me." Why was I holding my breath when I said that?

Kip shrugged. "I love the game."

Somehow that wasn't the answer I was hoping for.

fifteen

I was trying to focus on our pre-game warm up and not think about how bad Friday night's game had been. Despite our epic loss, Coach Helen showed up at our Monday morning practice and acted like we hadn't totally bombed that last game. Mind you, her practice notes seemed to have grown to several pages, including plenty of passing and shooting drills. She had commented that my passing had improved by leaps and bounds, and it made me smile.

This was our last game before the Christmas break and I, for one, wanted to finally make a good impression on her.

"Look who's watching us," Rachel said as she stood next to me in the arc around Sam, waiting for our turn to shoot on the net.

I glanced up into the stands. The Three Stooges grinned back at me. Only this time there were five.

They had brought some friends. Didn't those guys have anything better to do other than sitting there, gawking at us. Like homework? Where was a major assignment when you needed it? Ugh.

There were actually some other spectators in the stands. Maybe we were finally getting noticed? On the other hand, maybe they belonged to the other team, the Vipers or Asps or snakey-something-or-others.

Rachel took the face-off. I was positioned on the edge of the circle beside a girl even shorter than me. Just before the ref dropped the puck, I heard a strange noise.

Did she just growl at me?

That marked the beginning of a truly bizarre game. Because of scheduling difficulties early in the season, this was the first time we had faced this team. I don't know what their problem was, but they went nuts on us from the first whistle.

"What is this," Rachel asked to me on the bench, chugging some water, "a hockey game or roller derby on ice?"

"Have you met the one who thinks she's a dog? She's been growling at me the whole time," I said.

Jenna leaned forward. "Do you mean that short girl?"
I nodded.

"You know, I'm glad she had a cage on, otherwise I think she would have tried to nip me!"

Now, I admit I'm not up on all the details of hockey rules, but I'm pretty sure canine behaviour is not allowed.

The fact that we scored a goal in the first period only seemed to incite their fury even further. Andrea got shoved in front of our bench so hard that she almost somersaulted right into us.

The ref blew his whistle and you should have heard them. They were practically howling with indignation, and the one who had done the shoving claimed Andrea had tripped her, elbowed her, sworn at her—you name it, Andrea supposedly did it.

The ref, who looked young and unsure, talked it over with the linesman and then gave both girls a penalty.

Coach Helen called the ref over.

"Mr. Percy, is it?" She flashed him a smile. "Now, I know that you can't watch every player every moment, but I'm sure if you think back over the last few minutes of play you will realize that not only did my player not trip anyone, but she was the victim of interference."

The coach on the other bench walked closer to hear what was going on.

"The call was tripping. The call stands," the ref said, glancing quickly at the other coach.

Coach Helen clasped her hands in front of her. I wondered if she was going to start praying.

"Mr. Percy." Coach Helen wasn't smiling anymore. "The Good Lord gave you eyes to see the game, ears to hear what's going on around you, and a mouth to blow your whistle. Now perhaps you could put those gifts to good use and CALL A FAIR GAME."

Her voice carried across the ice and made the linesman standing by the penalty box snicker. The ref reddened, his eyes flashed, and he skated away.

We wanted to fight back but Coach Helen kept insisting

we play a game of skill. It was hard to concentrate on passing and stick handling when those snake girls were running over us like steamrollers.

The Growler seemed to have a personal grudge against me. I couldn't figure out why...I didn't even know her.

We lost the game four to two, and even our second goal was bitterly contested by the other team. They were pretty sore when the ref allowed it. Growler skated over to me and said in a low voice, "This isn't over, pretty girl."

I skated away pretending I hadn't heard her. She didn't know it, but she was lucky she wasn't saying stuff like that to Rachel. Nun or no nun, Rachel would have been all over her like hot fudge on a sundae.

"How many more games against them do we have?" Andrea asked after the final whistle, still fuming about her unearned penalty.

"I think two," I answered, dreading both of them.

"Girls?" Coach Helen poked her head in. "Everyone decent?"

"Come in," Jenna said.

Coach Helen looked at our faces. "I know this was a tough game, but you made me proud. Sister Louise and Sister Kate were pretty impressed with your self-discipline and commitment to the game."

More nuns?

"Are they your roomies?" Jenna asked.

"Yup."

Rachel leaned over to me and lowered her voice, "The

one looked like a truck driver and the other a librarian."

I had to really try not to giggle.

"And even though we don't always agree with the ref..." Helen continued.

There were mutterings from around the room.

"...it's all part of the game. I had heard through the grapevine that this team was a bit of a nightmare, but we handled it. It's not easy to take the high road, but we don't want to sink to their level."

"The high road is a great place to be when you don't have to worry about being a Hornet's hot tamale," Rachel said as we all gathered up our gear.

"A Hornet's hot tamale?" Coach Helen asked. "Does this have something to do with why I see some of the Hornets' players are at most of our games?"

Lilly spoke up. "Well, we sorta made this bet with them."

Coach Helen raised her eyebrows. "What kind of bet?"

"Whichever team has the highest league standing at the end of the regular season, wins."

"And the losing team..?"

"Has to be the cheerleading squad for the winning team all next season."

Coach Helen let out a low whistle. "And by 'hot tamales' I assume the guys will want you to look, uh, hot?"

We nodded glumly.

"And you agreed to this?" Coach Helen sighed. "Girls, do any of you know why nuns traditionally wear habits?"

No one answered.

"It's because our world has a language of signs. The

clothes we wear are just one way of sending a message about who we are and what we believe. If you're looking for dignity and respect, I don't think 'hot tamale' outfits are the way to go."

"But we made the bet already," Lilly said.

"Right. Then let's just make sure you win it. So who's up for an extra practice this week?"

Every hand in the room went up.

We gathered our gear and headed out. As we rounded the corner to the lobby we came to a halt. The snake team was blocking the whole area, a sea of smug faces.

"Tell me they're not waiting for us," Rachel said through gritted teeth.

I sure hoped they weren't. There was only so much self-control in Rachel on any given day and she had used it all up during the game. One word now and she'd go off like a rocket.

"Excuse me," I said to the girl near me so sweetly I would probably get diabetes. I elbowed my way through the snake girls trying not to let my hockey bag hit them *too* hard.

"Tara, hold on a minute," Coach Helen called to me.

I guess as I swung around, my bag hit Growler in the arm. You'd think I had just levelled her with a wrecking ball the way she carried on.

"Sorry, didn't mean to..." was all I got out before I felt myself being yanked backward and down.

What happened next is a bit of a blur for me, seeing as I was on the ground with fists and feet aiming for my face and chest. I was really scared. I've heard of people getting trampled to death in crowds.

After what seemed like years, I heard Coach Helen's voice in my ear, "Get up, Tara. I've got you."

I struggled to my feet. The truck driver nun had Growler in some sort of headlock.

"Now just calm down," she was saying to Growler.

"How'd she do that?" I asked Helen. Growler was totally incapacitated and the nun hadn't even broken a sweat.

"Sister Louise is a second degree black belt in karate. She says it comes in handy when she counsels youth at the Lambden Correction Centre."

"I'M GONNA SUE!" Growler screamed.

The tall nun looked unperturbed. "That so? Sister Kate, has this little wildcat got a case?"

The little nun shook her head. "The law clearly states that reasonable force can be used to prevent the commission of a serious offence that would be likely to cause immediate and serious injury or property damage."

I looked at Coach Helen, incredulous.

"Sister Kate was a paralegal before she joined the order," Coach Helen whispered.

I was just grateful that the Hornets weren't there to witness the scene. That's all I'd need: news to race around school that I got into a fight and was rescued by a bunch of nuns. Never mind that one was my coach and the other two were straight out of *The Karate Kid* and *Law & Order*.

Sister Louise released Growler and the snake team

filed out to board their bus, but not before looking back at us with hate in their eyes.

Oh yeah. Those next two games against them were going to be fun.

sixteen

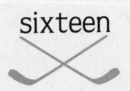

Winter Break is a crock. The teachers get a break from us, but we certainly don't get a break from school work. I had a culminating activity and two papers to write. But at least there were no classes for two weeks and besides, Christmas was coming. I had asked for new hockey gloves. The ones I had been using were hand-me-downs from Will, and not only were they a bit too big, but no amount of baking soda, anti-odor sprays, or air fresheners could get rid of the stink.

"Aunt Tabitha called this afternoon," Stephan said to Mom as she put a plate of ribs on the table.

I wasn't particularly hungry, but we always ate early on Tuesday nights because that was my mom's bridge night.

"She wants to know if you want her seashell lamp."

"Why would I want that hideous thing? I'd have nightmares with that in the house."

Stephan shrugged. "She's moving to Costa Rica on one of those eco-missions."

"What is it this time?" my dad asked. "The Michigan Monkey flower, the Rodrigues fruit bat, the wild yak?"

"The Harris Rice Water Rat."

My mother paused, balancing a potato on a spoon in mid air. "A rat that lives in the water?"

"It's endangered."

"I would hope so," Mom said.

"Tara," Dad said, "don't forget we have the pancake breakfast tomorrow."

I had forgotten about the Rotary Club's annual Christmas breakfast. My dad and I helped every year by filling plates with steaming hot pancakes and sausage and gooey maple syrup for everyone in town.

"Sorry, Dad, but I have a practice in the morning."

Coach Helen had somehow managed to snag us a humane practice time. I don't think we had ever skated in daylight before.

My dad's face fell. "You're really not coming? Because of a hockey practice?"

I stared at him. Hockey practice in our house was almost a sacred rite. Practice times went on the family calendar in blue ink (games in red) and everything else in our lives was slotted in around them in pencil. I had added my practices to the calendar myself, so it shouldn't have been a surprise to him.

"But you've always said that 'Championships are won at practice,'" I said.

"Well yes, but..."

"But what? Take Will with you. He's free and he's never, ever helped at one of those."

"Me? Why me?" Will looked as if he had been asked to clean out sewers or something. "I don't want to slop breakfast food all morning."

"Why not you?" I sputtered. "You've got two arms."

Will opened his mouth to whine some more.

"It's all right, Will," my dad said, putting his hand on Will's shoulder. "I'll go by myself."

Oh, don't even try the guilt thing on me, I thought. How many times had I had to take an extra turn at dishes so Stephan or Will could get to their games or practices on time?

I jumped up from the table.

"Where are you going, Tara?" my mom asked.

"I have a meeting," I said. "I'll be home before it's dark."

I stomped out of the room, making sure I slammed the front door on my way out. I was so sick of the double standard in our house. It occurred to me that Mom could try saying something to stick up for us women, for a change.

My hockey bag banged into my right hip as I made my way over to Kip's pond. I had found a shortcut through the fields that made it only a fifteen minute walk from my house, even in the snow.

Kip was just lacing up when I arrived.

"You look like you're ready to clobber someone," he said, a slight look of alarm on his face.

"I am."

"I'm sorry."

"For what? I'm not mad at you."

"Oh, OK. I just thought I should apologize just in case."

I tried not to, but I couldn't help smiling. "It's my family," I said. "For my brothers, it's hockey this and hockey that, and for me, it's 'Tara, can you be our maid so the boys can play?' And when I have to miss one tiny thing because of a practice, I get the 'guilt look.'"

Kip nodded. "Oh, I know that look well. Only I get it if I even hint that I might miss a practice because I'm not feeling well, or heaven forbid, need to study for an exam. And don't even think about missing a game. You should have heard my dad arguing with the doctor to let me back on the ice only a week after the concussion. Dr. Chan was having none of it. Given the chance, I'm sure my dad would wheel me out onto the ice on a stretcher or tape my hockey stick to a cast before he let me miss a game."

Kip hobbled onto the ice, dragging his right leg behind him. "I'm coming, Dad," he cried dramatically, "just let me duct tape this other foot back in place."

"You should join the drama club," I called.

He skated back, a look of mock horror on his face. "And... miss... hockey practice?" he said, clutching his heart and falling backwards into the snow bank.

I couldn't help it—I laughed. Maybe my family wasn't the most annoying after all.

"Come on," he said. "Let's put that anger to good use. We'll work on slap shots today."

"You mean I can vent my anger on a poor defenceless piece of rubber?"

"Absolutely. Best therapy ever."

He let me fire away until his bucket of pucks was empty. To his credit, I did feel a bit better afterwards.

He collected all the pucks and brought the bucket back to where I was standing.

"You got quite a few of them in the net, but you need a little work on your technique. And once you shoot the puck, stop twisting your body like you can make it curve into the net or something. Once the puck leaves your stick, it's out of your control. All you can do is wait to see what happens next."

He showed me where to place the puck, how far back to swing and how to shift my weight.

"Not bad, not bad. But you need to close your stick on the follow-through."

I had no idea what he was talking about, but it turned out it had to do with rolling my wrists again. Was it wrong of me to be happy that I was going to need another hands-on demonstration? I found myself hoping that every skill in hockey involved wrist-rolling.

Kip stood behind me and showed me what he meant. I couldn't help leaning back into that strong chest. Unfortunately that little lean put me off balance, and as I fought to get my skates under me again, I clipped Kip under the chin with my elbow. We fell to the ice in a tangled heap of sticks and skates.

I was only inches away from his face. The look of surprise on his face was replaced with a look I had never seen before...like he was going to kiss me.

Just as he moved a bit closer we heard them. Voices.

Male voices coming down the lane from Kip's house to the pond.

We scrambled to free ourselves. It involved a lot of struggling and cursing. When the guys rounded the pines near the pond I was sitting on the little wooden bench taking off my skates while Kip violently practised his slap shot.

Tyler, Braydon, and a couple other players stopped short when they saw me. They looked from Kip to me and back to Kip.

Yeah, this wasn't at all awkward.

"Little private practice?" Tyler said with a leer.

I tossed my head. "Hardly. I'm just trying to break in some new skates." Tyler's eyes moved to the well-worn skates I was rapidly shoving into my hockey bag. His eyebrows raised.

"They're new to me," I added, wanting to smack my own forehead. Why, oh, why could I not lie better under pressure? No one needs to break in used skates.

I walked away with as much dignity as I could muster.

seventeen

Between the extra practices and my schoolwork, the two weeks flew by and I felt ready to pick up where we left off in the league schedule. I had worked with Kip five or six times over the break. He wasn't kidding when he said he was on the pond almost every day. After the slap shot session he seemed careful not to end up tangled on the ice with me again, though. I had to wonder how much ribbing he had endured from the guys. We also had three intense practices with Coach Helen.

At our last practice before the break was over, Coach Helen floored us by saying, "Oh, by the way girls, our next game start time is now on Wednesday at 7:30."

A game before 10 pm?

"Wow," Sam said. "How'd you manage that?"

Coach Helen smiled. "I have friends in high places."

"Do you mean..." Sam pointed with her index finger skyward, "the 'Big Guy'?"

"No," Coach Helen said, her forehead creasing. "I

mean I have an uncle on the Minor Hockey Board of Directors."

"Oh. Yeah." Sam blushed slightly. "I guess that works, too."

It seemed I wasn't the only one ready to face the new year. Despite the added pressure of first-semester exam season, we pulled together like the championship team we were, took our next three games, and climbed to third place. It felt good to be going up in the standings again.

Sister Louise and Sister Kate were also regulars in the stands now. Was it wrong of me to feel relieved that if we needed some protection, a nun had our backs?

"I was right about the Hornets, wasn't I?" Rachel asked, diving into her turkey club sandwich, a Burger Bar specialty.

"Right about what?" I asked, moving over to make room in our booth for Lilly and Grace who had just shown up. Sam slid in beside Rachel and Jenna.

"The Hornets have dropped one game and tied another. They've fallen to third place." Rachel smiled triumphantly.

"So we're tied with them in league standings?" Andrea asked. "Very nice."

"Lilly, what are you doing with that knife?" Jenna asked, eying her with concern.

Lilly stopped arcing her butter knife in the air. "Well, I'm trying to work out where the best place is to stab someone."

We all took that in for a moment.

"With an ice knife."

"Oh! Your novel," I said, relieved.

"Of course. I've come across a problem with it. See, the body's normal temperature is about 98 degrees, right?"

"Right," I said.

"Well, after even one plunge, the ice blade will melt pretty fast. So I need to make the first strike lethal." She looked around the table, a little glint in her eye.

"Up under the rib cage, straight into the heart," Andrea stated, matter-of-factly. "Add a twist just to be sure."

Lilly was nodding.

Sam shook her head. "Carotid artery. He'll bleed out in two minutes." She made a slashing motion with her hand across her neck.

"Too messy," Rachel said. "Is he attacking from the front or the back?"

"Front," Lilly said.

"If he gets in close, fast, you won't be able to get your hand up in time," Rachel said. She stood up and pulled Lilly up to face her to demonstrate. "See, the knife is trapped in my hand by my side." She took the butter knife and brought it around behind Lilly to her back. "Up into the liver. He'll drop like a stone."

We were seriously impressed. And more than a little disturbed. Exactly what kind of programs were they showing on the Discovery Channel?

"Working on game strategy to beat the Greys?" a voice asked. We didn't even have to turn around to know it was Tyler.

The Three Stooges stood by our booth, grinning.

"Maybe it's you guys who need a game strategy,"

Rachel said. "Dropping in the standings, I hear."

Braydon scoffed. "One place isn't dropping. It's a... fluctuation. And we can get that back in a couple of games."

Rachel shrugged. "We seem to be on a winning streak."

Tyler spoke to everyone but looked in my direction. "Must be all that practising you're doing."

I squirmed in my seat. Would Tyler say anything about finding me at the pond that day? I hadn't done anything wrong, I reasoned, but I really didn't feel like being grilled by everyone about the relationship. Especially seeing as I wasn't really sure there was one.

"Did you hear that Cartwright is hosting the Midget Western Conference Tournament in few weeks?" Kip asked quickly. "It's gonna bring a lot of hockey scouts and bigwigs into town."

"I thought that tournament was being held in Winterton?" Grace asked.

"Didn't you hear? Their arena caught fire two days ago," Tyler said. "It's still standing but there was a lot of damage. Something to do with the chip fryer in the concession booth. Nearly took the whole building with it."

I felt bad for the residents of Winterton. All the old arenas around here, including ours, were made almost entirely of wood. It only took a tiny spark to turn one into a giant weenie roast.

At least our league didn't play in Winterton, so it wouldn't affect us.

Or so I thought.

eighteen

The news shocked us into complete silence.

"What do you mean we have to forfeit? *All* our games? But we're in third place!"

Coach Helen clasped her hands in front of her. "Our ice time has been cut. That means no more practice ice, and the only slot available for games is 11 pm Sunday night. I phoned the other coaches, but their teams aren't willing to travel that late at night, especially in the winter."

"But what happened to our ice times?"

Coach Helen sighed. "This Midget Tournament is the priority. There are a *lot* of teams coming and their game schedules come first."

"But that's weeks away!" I said.

"Yes, but it has pushed all the other teams' schedules forward and in the end, it was decided that there wasn't room for our team."

"But there are still three weeks left in the season! Can't

someone do something?" Rachel asked.

"I've asked Kate to look into it." Coach Helen leaned out the door and called Kate and Louise in. Kate had a sheaf of papers in her hand. We looked at her with hopeful eyes, but her face was grim. Her first words were *not* what we wanted to hear.

"Legally, they can do this."

We all groaned.

"But it will cost them. They'll lose the money they paid as our 'performance bond' and there will be fines to the league. I went to talk to the league president and used that as leverage to help convince him to find a solution that allows you to keep playing." She pulled out one of the papers. "I've made some recommendations regarding extending hours for the arena..." Out came a chart. "...a more streamlined use of maintenance staff and a proposal to reschedule some students' spares to allow early afternoon practice."

She stopped and looked up.

"Well?" I asked, unable to stand the suspense. "What did he say?"

"He said he would 'take it under consideration' and then I was escorted out of his office."

Another round of groans. Kate gave Coach Helen an 'I'm sorry' look and they left.

"This can't be happening," Sam said. "I just figured out how to 'butterfly.'" She threw her blocker into the corner.

"What about your uncle on the Board of Directors?" I asked.

Coach Helen shook her head. "I tried, but the convener

was adamant that the boys not lose any of their ice time."

The convener again. Why did that guy always seem to be at the root of our troubles?

"How about Julian Falls?" Jenna asked. "Could we get some ice time there? Just to finish the season?"

More head shaking. "All available ice time there is being offered to the teams from Winterton."

We slouched on the benches in the dressing room for what was now going to be our last game.

Saturday morning I tried to bury my sorrows under an avalanche of apple turnovers, a pecan butter tart, and a nainamo bar. At this rate, I wasn't going to fit into my softball uniform in the summer.

I walked home slowly, trying to get rid of most of the evidence before I got "that look" from my mother. I was almost there when I saw Kip coming in the opposite direction.

His hands were in his pockets and he eyed my bag from Hannah's. I clutched it tight to my chest. Only the apple turnover was left, and nobody was getting their hands on it.

"Hi," he said. "You wanna come to the pond this afternoon?"

"I guess you haven't heard. We're done. The ice was pulled out from under us."

Kip looked down. "Yeah, I heard. That's a tough break. I just thought maybe you still wanted to play a bit."

I opened my mouth to say some smart remark, but Kip looked a bit miserable himself.

"I'll see," I said.

I continued home and went quietly in the front door, trying to avoid my mother. As I gently slipped my boots into the closet I heard an 'ahem' behind me. I jumped five feet in the air, at least.

"I can't believe I just saw that." It was Stephan, looking smug and superior.

"Just saw what?" I asked, holding the bakery bag behind my back.

"Just saw you talking to Kip, that's what."

I really didn't have the patience for Stephan's games. That apple turnover was calling my name.

"So?"

"Kip *Russell.*"

I stared at him uncomprehendingly.

"As in the son of the convener, Mr. *Russell,*" Stephan said. He walked away shaking his head. "I was sure he was the *last* person you'd ever talk to after what his dad did to your team."

I ran upstairs, threw the bag with the turnover on my bed, and stormed out of the house. I did go to the pond, but not with any gear. Besides it was probably dangerous for me to be on the pond right now. I was so hot with anger that the ice would have melted under my skates.

Kip looked up as I approached and gave me a wide smile.

Oh yeah, buddy, I thought. *Let's see if you're still smiling when I'm through with you.*

"You forgot your gear."

"Oh yeah," I yelled, marched right onto the ice with my boots. "Like you *forgot* to tell me who your father is!"

Kip moved backward, his face flushed.

"What's the big deal?" he said, not very convincingly.

"Well, let's see Kip *Russell*. The big deal is your father, Mr. *Russell*, has been a thorn in our sides from the beginning. You knew what he was doing with Mr. Santos!" I pounded a fist on his shoulder. Kip didn't move.

"You knew what was happening with our ice time!" I pounded again. My hand bounced off his shoulder. "You never said a word! And all this time I thought you were so nice, helping me. You...you *traitor*!"

Kip's cheeks were red.

"Tara," he said.

I shot him fierce look and started stomping away across the ice. No way was I sticking around to hear his excuses. He skated after me and pulled on my arm.

"Look, I knew that if I told you, you'd think I could do something. But he wouldn't have listened to me anyway. It doesn't matter what I say to him—he looks right through me."

"I'll bet you didn't even try," I said to him.

"It wouldn't have made a difference!" Kip said, throwing his stick on the ground. "He *never* listens to me."

"Oh, poor baby hockey star," I said. "It's terrible that you are so talented and forced to follow your dream. Do you even know what it's like to have someone else telling you what you can and cannot do?"

Kip got quiet. "As a matter of fact I do. I've told my dad in a thousand different ways that I don't want a career in hockey. I want to study mechanical engineering. Might as well be telling him I want to be a chicken plucker. He keeps pushing me to go straight to the OHL so I have a better chance at playing pro. I want to play Junior A so I can get a real hockey scholarship down the road. He just brushes it off like it's a phase I'm going through and keeps talking about tryouts for hockey camps and invites scouts to watch my games."

"But, you're so good at hockey. You told me you love the game."

"I do love hockey. But not as my job. It's a pretty unstable business and besides..." He smiled wryly. "I wouldn't mind keeping all my brain cells."

I tried not to feel for him. This was supposed to be *my* pity party. But he did look pretty miserable. Cute, but miserable.

"Still," I said, "you could put your foot down and insist. He can't force you to play professionally."

"No," Kip agreed. "But it will be World War III in our house. I'm just biding my time and enjoying playing until I actually have to fill out the applications down the road. Then I'll face him."

"See, that's the difference right there. You still have control over what is happening to you. We're at the mercy of the 'boys club' in town." I looked up at him. "I really thought you guys would be the first to stick up for us. You talk about loving the game—I mean, you goaded us into playing with this stupid dare, even! But now when they're cutting us, you disappear. I guess you only love that *you* get to play."

"That's not fair, Tara! No one asked us if we thought it was right or not. We didn't even know until it was all over."

"Oh, it's not over," I snapped. "We're not going away quietly."

Kip smiled. "I'm glad to hear it."

"Are you really? Then *help* us. Talk to your dad, at least."

"I told you. It wouldn't make any difference."

"Maybe not," I said. "But it would make a difference to me."

nineteen

"This is so totally wrong," Rachel said, her eyes smouldering with anger. "They should take ice time away from all the teams equally. Not shut us down so the boys won't have their precious schedules interrupted."

"Oh, but *they're* all headed to the NHL, doncha know?" sneered Sam.

We chomped our fries in silence. It really was a bit hard to take. When it came right down to it, the men in town only tolerated us as long as we didn't inconvenience the "important" sports teams. It was not unlike how it was at home. My parents came to my softball games only if there was nothing else on the schedule. And forget practices altogether. We were alone on the field. And now the same with our hockey team. It didn't matter what sport we played or how well we did, we girls were always second best.

We were so close to finishing the season and beating

the guys, who were barely holding onto third place. But I bet they would still make us pay up the debt. I tried to picture myself in black spandex kicking up my legs while I shouted: *Go, Hornets!* Just the thought of it made my stomach do a backflip of its own.

"We can't just take this lying down," I said, pounding my fist on the table. "We have to take a stand."

"And just how are we supposed to do that?" Jenna asked. "Coach Helen has already petitioned the Board. They turned her down flat. Even her uncle couldn't help her. He told her the decision was made, and she should forget about it."

"We can't let the men of this town get away with this," Rachel said.

"Or the women," I added. "How many of them are fighting for a chance for their daughters to play hockey? Practically none."

There were nods all around.

"Yeah, the Minor Hockey Association would just love us to slink away and accept it because we're girls," Andrea said.

"We have to keep this front and centre so every man in town is reminded of how they let us down," Sam said.

"What about a billboard?" Lilly offered.

"Too expensive," I said.

"Radio ad?"

"The only people who listen to the local station are the farmers for the crop report."

A gust of wind blew our serviettes off the table. In

came George, carrying a cardboard box. He set it on the counter.

"Hi, George," I called over.

"Drowning your sorrows in fries?" he asked, grinning.

"You heard, huh?"

George nodded.

"What's that in the box?"

George pulled out a Burger Bar T-shirt. "Al's T-shirt order. Whatcha think?" He held it up so we could see what was printed on the back.

Harassing the server will definitely *result in smaller portions.*

"That's hilarious!" I said, laughing.

We needed a good laugh right about now. George handed the box to Al who slipped a size XXL shirt over his head. He gave us a big toothy grin.

"Hey, is anyone else thinking what I'm thinking?" I asked, my eyes fixed on the T-shirt.

"That Al needs to start eating at Wanda's Wheat Grass and More?"

"No. I mean the T-shirts. Great place for a message, don't you think?"

"Tara, you're brilliant," Rachel said. "T-shirts are even better than billboards. We can wear them everywhere and really spread the word."

"Yeah, but what are we going to put on them?" Sam asked. "It has to be something that will make people think about how unfair this is."

"How about 'Hustle and heart set us apart'?" Lilly said.

"'United we play, United we win'?" Andrea offered.

Rachel shook her head.

"I think they're pretty good," I said.

"It's not the words that are wrong, it's that *there are words.*"

"So what?"

"If we have *any* slogan, we won't be able to wear them in school," Rachel said. "And I think it's really important to show everyone, especially the boys' hockey teams, that we are ticked off. School is where they'll have maximum exposure."

"Shoot, she's right," Sam said. "So what do we use? A picture?"

"I think I know the perfect thing," I said, having a rare lightbulb moment. "Let's go see George."

George put a rush on our order and the shirts were ready for Monday. I looked at my navy blue T-shirt with the big symbol on the front in the mirror before I left for school. It was perfect. No words, but the message was clear; we are equal.

"Even Principal Tuttle can't veto this," Lilly said, meeting me at my locker in her new purple T-shirt. "There is no ban on symbols." She waved and headed to class.

The large equal sign on the front of each of our T-shirts couldn't be missed. Or misunderstood.

"What are these T-shirts you're wearing?" Tyler asked, catching up with me in the hall on the way to

English. "Some new math club?"

OK, so it could be misunderstood by Neanderthal hockey players.

"Funny, Tyler," I said, trying desperately not to roll my eyes. "It means exactly what it looks like it means."

He squinted at my chest. Oh great. Maybe the placement of the equal sign wasn't that well thought out. I should have had it stamped on the *back* of my shirt.

"Equal, Tyler. E-q-u-a-l." I tried saying it slowly so he would get it.

"What's equal?" Braydon and Kip had come up behind Tyler and now all three of them were staring at my chest. That's it. I was going to have to wear my shirt backwards from now on.

"We're equal," I said, making a circle with my hand that encompassed all of us standing there. "You know... girls...and guys."

They gave me blank stares.

"Does this have something to do with the hockey schedule?" Braydon finally asked.

I was kept from smacking him on the forehead by the arrival of Rachel, Sam, and Lilly.

"Of course it does," Rachel said, overhearing. "Hey, by the way, I heard that your team's practice times are being cut in half so the juniors can have more ice time."

Rachel had heard no such thing, but I didn't say anything. I knew what she was doing. It was going to take an example that hit close to home for the guys to understand how we felt.

"The juniors!" Tyler was outraged. "They couldn't win

a game even if the other team didn't show up. We're supposed to give up our ice time so they can play more? That's not right!"

The four of us said nothing, but just folded our arms and stared.

Kip was the first to speak up. "Our ice time isn't being cut, guys. The girls are just trying to make a point." Then he bowed. "And it worked."

"So are you going to speak to your dad?" I asked, raising my eyebrows.

Kip looked down at his feet.

I turned and left. Typical Kip: gorgeous dark eyes, cute mouth, strong arms, and no backbone.

twenty

"You know you all look ridiculous," the blonde-haired, model-thin, designer-jeans-wearing snit standing by our table in the cafeteria said in her high-pitched 'everyone look at me' voice.

"Shut your yap, Vicki," Rachel said. "You're no better off than we are."

"What do you mean by that?" Vicki asked, tossing her immaculately straight hair over a shoulder with a quick glance around the room to see who was watching. "I didn't get pushed around by the boys. In fact," she said with another look around the room and a quick smile at the jocks in the corner, "the boys usually make way for me."

I choked on my bun.

"Really?" Rachel said, raising an eyebrow. "Ever wonder why your aquafit class got moved back to 7:30 in the freezing o'clock morning last year?"

The smirk disappeared off Vicki's face. "They said it was the only time our instructor could come."

Rachel shook her head. "Nuh-uh. It's because the *men's* water polo team was gearing up for the provincial championships, and Kurt Bruder refused to practice without first having his kelp smoothie from Wanda's, and she doesn't open until eight."

A pout formed on Vicki's cherry-sparkle lip-glossed lips. "But that's not fair! It was so cold that early in the morning that I had to wear my one-piece suit instead of my new bikini."

Rachel put a hand to her mouth. "The horror!"

Vicki, not even registering the sarcasm, nodded violently. "And when I got out," she lowered her voice to a whisper, "I had to put on a polyester terry robe to warm up. *Polyester!*"

Rachel *tsked* sympathetically, and took another sip of her chocolate milk.

Vicki put both hands on the table and leaned down to Rachel, her eyes black dots of anger. "Where do I get my T-shirt?"

It was sort of strange to have anything at all in common with the plastic girls. But I have to tell you, when they get behind something, they go all out. Dolores told me that so many orders for equal-sign T-shirts came in that George worked almost around the clock to keep up. Equal T-shirts popped all over school, in every grade. I wondered at first if all the girls were wearing them just to be plastic girl clones or because it was now considered the politically correct thing to do. But then again, I would bet that there wasn't one girl in town who hadn't been affected by the 'boys first' mentality.

"Are you gonna wear that stupid thing every day?" Will asked at the dinner table, wrinkling his nose.

I looked down at my Equal T-shirt. "Stupid?" I said. "I'll tell you what's stupid; thinking that the girls' teams don't deserve to use the city's arenas and parks as much as the guys."

Will just made a face.

"Look, Tara," my dad said, "the fact is the guys have a chance to make a career out of this. For you girls, it's just a hobby."

I was almost speechless. My own father was one of them! I prepared to launch into a scathing verbal attack.

"Women's hockey has a national team you know, Bill," my mother said.

There was silence around the table. Mom usually distanced herself from hockey talk.

"They've won gold or silver at every international competition they've ever entered."

"Marion," Dad began in a voice that was a little too condescending, "you can't compare that to the NHL."

"A girl has a better chance of making it to the National Team than a boy does of making it into the NHL. On those statistics alone we should be letting all the girls play and cutting the boys' ice times back."

My dad's mouth hung open.

"Not to mention that the city seems to have no trouble taking taxes from every working woman in town to help pay for the arenas, parks, and ball diamonds. Why then shouldn't the women have equal access?"

She stood up and unbuttoned her sweater and took it off. I almost had tears in my eyes when I saw what she was wearing underneath. A hot pink T-shirt with a glittery gold equal sign stamped in the middle.

"Marion!" my dad sputtered. "Where did you get *that*?"

"I had George Wilton make it for me."

"You're—you're not going to wear that around town... are you?"

"I most certainly am. I promised the girls on our bridge team. We're a little tired of having to hold our meetings in the dingy, claustrophobic basement of the Moose Lodge while the men are comfortable in the large airy room on the main floor where the bathrooms are. We're lobbying to have equal time upstairs."

Stephan turned on me with a look of horror on his face. "Now see what you've done!"

I smiled at my mother, and she smiled back.

"Yes, I see," I said.

twenty-one

"Did you guys happen to see the ladies at Vern's Market?" Rachel asked, arriving breathless at our table in the cafeteria. "They're all wearing green Equal shirts under their aprons."

"That's great news!" Sam exclaimed.

I forced a smile. "Yeah, great." I munched on my sandwich.

"Tara?" Rachel said, sitting next to me. "What's wrong?"

I gave up on the smile. "They're a great idea. The T-shirts, I mean. But really, where are they getting us?"

The table went silent.

"Well, the word is getting out," Sam said. "Nadine from the Social Justice club interviewed me yesterday wanting to know details about the situation and what people can do to help. Her mom works for the Cartwright Herald and thinks maybe they'll run an article about it. And they're all wearing Equal T-shirts, of course."

"I know. Even my mom is wearing one," I said. "But it's been a week and half, and even though the message is spreading, we're no closer to getting our ice time back. We're running out of time to play double-headers to make up the missed games."

"I don't think they even have double-headers in hockey," sighed Sam.

"So, what are we supposed to do?" Lilly asked.

"I don't know," I said, miserably. "All I know is my dad saw the agenda for the Minor Hockey Board of Directors' meeting tomorrow night. And we're not on it. They don't care that the whole town knows what they've done. The only people protesting are the women and we all know what they think of us."

"Tara's right," Lilly admitted. "I overheard Mr. Russell in Hannah's bakery yesterday bragging about some big-time scout coming to the midget tournament. Dolores asked him what happened to the girls' team and he just shrugged and said that they had to keep their 'priorities.'"

"Even if every girl in town wore a T-shirt, we still wouldn't be a 'priority,'" I said.

"Well then, ladies, I think it's time we applied some pressure," Rachel said with that pitbull look in her eyes again. "I think it's time *we* became a priority."

"How're we going to do that?" Sam asked.

"If they don't care that the whole town knows, then we need to make this bigger than Cartwright," Rachel said. "Tell the team to meet at the Board of Directors' meeting tomorrow night."

"What are you going to do, Rachel?" I asked, feeling a little nervous.

"Put on your makeup, girls. I'm calling the media."

"The TV station in Julian Falls?"

"Yup."

"How are you going to get them to come?" I asked.

"My oldest sister interned there last year. They loved her and she still has a lot of contacts. I think she dated the weather guy."

"What about Coach Helen? Do you think she'll be mad?" Sam asked.

"I'll run it by her in case she was thinking of going to the meeting to plead our case again. We don't want to look disorganized—like the left hand doesn't know what the right hand is doing," Rachel said. "Let's get out there and spread the word. We want as many people out supporting us as possible."

I don't know what had my stomach in knots more...the thought that the Board would freak out at us for pulling this stunt, that the TV station wouldn't be on our side, or that I had to wear makeup.

I headed down the hall for English class, lost in thought about what kind of eye shadow I should wear. Heck, did I even own any eye shadow? So it wasn't surprising that I smacked into someone as I rounded the corner.

"Oh, sorry," I mumbled, looking down at my nails. Should I paint them?

"Just the hockey girl I was looking for," a voice said. Kip's voice.

"Why is it I always seem to run into you? Literally, I mean," I asked.

He smiled a dazzlingly handsome smile. "Fate."

"Probably more like disorientation."

"I was thinking about our conversation from the other day," he said.

Oh, brilliant. I was trying to remember if I owned makeup and he was testing my memory recall.

"Right. Our conversation."

"So I thought maybe I could, you know, help out another way."

Oh, *that* conversation. The one about how he wouldn't even speak to his father for us.

"What other way?"

As an answer, Kip began unzipping his jacket.

"Get *out*!" I said as he opened it up. "You're wearing an Equal T-shirt!"

"Yup. But in a manly black colour."

He was getting strange looks from the kids passing him in the hall, but to his credit he took the jacket off completely.

I was pretty impressed. He was in for a heap of teasing, starting right now. Tyler and Braydon had just spotted us.

"Hey, Kip," Tyler said, walking over and then stopped abruptly when he saw the T-shirt. "What. Is. That?"

Kip didn't answer.

"Soooo," Braydon said slowly, "You're like, going over to their side?"

"I'm not going to any side," Kip said. "That's the whole point of this. They're not lower than us, we're not higher; they're not over there and we're over here. We're equal. Get it?"

"Oh, we get it, Kip. And I guess we're not surprised. Seems you'll do anything to get the girl, huh?"

"Oh, evolve already, you Neanderthal," I said.

"Well, think about this," Kip told them. "My dad's been having an awful lot of phone conversations about bringing a Junior A team here to Cartwright."

"That would be awesome!" Tyler exclaimed.

"What? You think having a top level team in town isn't going to affect *our* ice time?" Kip asked.

Now they looked worried.

"You might not know it, but this is our fight, too."

The warning bell rang. We had five minutes to get to class.

"We gotta go," Tyler said, shooting a look at me. He nudged Braydon on the arm and they left.

"Is that true about the Junior A team?" I asked Kip.

Kip nodded. "Although they might not come. Cartwright probably isn't big enough to support a team of that level. But it's a possibility."

"So are you wearing that shirt for us or for you?"

Kip grinned. "For all of us. We're equal, right? And my dad may not listen to what I say, but he can't really ignore what I'm wearing."

"Are you really going to wear it around your dad?"

He waited to answer until the final bell for class stopped clanging.

"Better than that," he said. "I'm going to wear it to the Board of Directors' meeting tomorrow night." He waved as he sprinted down the hall.

The meeting? Tomorrow night? Oh boy. His dad wasn't going to be the only one to see him wear his protest shirt.

twenty-two

We arrived at the meeting, armoured in our Equal T-shirts and ready to do battle.

I had been rehearsing for a good hour in front of the bathroom mirror what I would say if I was asked any questions by a reporter.

What do you think of the Minor Hockey Association cutting your ice time?

Well, Brian, (all news anchors seemed to be named Brian) I think the members of the Board of Directors have forgotten that we are first and foremost athletes and deserve the same opportunities as other players.

Who came up with this amazing idea of 'Equal' T-shirts?

(Modest laugh) Well, the T-shirts were a group idea, but I came up with the design.

So, what's next for this incredibly talented group of young women?

You know, Brian, we are ready to tackle anything that comes our way. But first we plan on finishing our hockey season at the top of our league, and then recapturing our title as softball champions next summer.

I was just thinking up a good response to the question of how it felt to be role models for thousands of girls across the country, when Stephan banged on the door asking how much longer I'd be and who I was talking to.

An hour later, Rachel and I made our way over to the Cozy Corner Inn where the hockey association held its meetings. We met up with the rest of the team in the parking lot and stormed the lobby. We threw our coats and hats in a heap on a chair and proudly displayed our shirts.

It was pandemonium inside. There were three or four different camera crews setting up their gear while reporters were trying to corner anyone who didn't look like hotel staff for a statement. I saw Nadine and the Social Justice crowd doing an interview and even some of the plastic girls milling around, although they looked more like they were participating in a photo shoot than a protest against inequality. Still, they were wearing the T-shirts.

But judging by the equipment, this looked like more than our local TV station. Mr. Taylor, head of the Minor Hockey Association, was trying to get things under control while wiping his forehead with his sleeve every few seconds. Now I know why men used to carry handkerchiefs. Mr. Taylor's sleeve looked like it could be wrung out—and the meeting hadn't even started yet.

I looked around to see if Kip had really shown up, but instead I caught a glimpse of Mr. Russell. He was shooting daggers out of his eyes at us. I stared back. We weren't the ones who had done anything wrong, after all. He broke off the staring contest first as something by the main doors caught his eye and a flicker of surprise raced across his face.

I didn't recognize her at first; she had never worn that black nun thing on her head before. Sister Helen and her Pious Posse had shown up wearing dark skirts, blue sweaters, cross necklaces, and their wimples. The nuns meant business.

"Hi, girls," she said, coming over to us. "Looks like we all had the same idea when we got dressed tonight." She smiled. "Oh, excuse me. I see the National News team has arrived. I want to thank them for coming."

"You called the National News?" I couldn't believe it. No wonder Mr. Russell and Mr. Taylor looked upset.

"Well, it's like they say," Sister Helen said, walking away. "Go big or go home."

"Here comes the backpedalling and double talk," Rachel whispered in my ear. A reporter was heading for Mr. Russell, a cameraman in tow.

"I hope they've got flame-resistant clothing on," I said. "Mr. Russell looks like he's about to explode."

"Serves him right," Sam said, overhearing our whispers. "He's like the evil mastermind behind all this."

"Mr. Taylor's the president, though," I said. "Doesn't he have the final word?"

"Are you kidding?" Rachel said. "Would you have the guts to stand up to Russell? Look at his face. He probably eats komodo dragons for breakfast."

Mr. Russell had his arms folded while he talked to the reporter and his face was like stone. I could see now why Kip wasn't too keen on arguing with him.

"Incoming!" Rachel said.

A reporter from CVTV was headed in our direction.

"Ladies!" the young woman with the microphone said. "I see you all wearing these T-shirts." I was closest so she shoved the mike in my face. "Can you tell me what they're all about?"

My mouth opened but nothing came out. All that rehearsing in front of the mirror and I was still tongue-tied.

Sam leaned forward. "It's just a way to remind the men of this town that we're equal."

The reporter turned to her cameraman. "Mark, get a close-up of the shirts." She smiled at the camera again, "The girls of this town are fighting for more than just their ice time. They want to be treated as equals both on and off the ice."

"And we're behind them," said a voice that sounded strangely like Tyler's. "We're all equal. Men and women."

I can't speak for everyone on our team, but I nearly fell over. The entire boys' midget team was there sporting Equal T-shirts.

"The men?" the reporter asked. "I thought this meeting

was about the girls' team being cut."

I felt the insane urge to giggle. If she only knew that the original agenda consisted of debate over whether to go with oranges or frozen muffin dough as fundraisers and a show of hands as to how many members would be available for a meeting during March Break.

"Well, you can't be equal by yourself," Braydon said.

"So, you support the girls' hockey team's fight for equal ice time?" she asked, signalling silently to Mark to get a wide shot of both the guys and the girls.

"We support the idea that all teams deserve equal ice or pitch or pool or diamond time."

"What about house leagues? Should they take ice time away from the travel teams?"

Those reporters are sneaky. She was trying to trip him up.

"It's not a matter of taking ice time away from anyone." Kip stepped forward, his face red but determined. "It's a matter of dividing the time equally among the teams."

"But why should the hobby players get as much access as the serious players...the guys who could go on in the sport?"

She looked innocent when she said it, but you could see she was trying to get a rise out of Kip.

Kip opened his mouth to answer and then hesitated. His dad and Mr. Taylor were standing just behind the camera. I had never seen someone look as angry as Mr. Russell.

"Because it's a great game. And everyone deserves to

play." Kip was answering the reporter, but he was looking at his dad.

"Even the girls?" the reporter tried one more time.

Kip smiled. "Especially the girls. Have you ever seen them play? They're great. And no wonder—in the off -season many of them play on a championship-winning softball team."

Oh, funny. Softball was now our 'off-season'. He was going to pay for that later.

The reporter swung around to Rachel and began asking her all about our team.

I watched Kip's dad turn and walk out of the lobby, not saying a word to anyone.

I moved over beside Kip. "Do you want me to go talk to him?" I said, feeling a bit responsible. After all, I was the one who had badgered him about standing up to his dad.

Kip shook his head. "It's a conversation that's long overdue." He smiled at me. "It'll be fine." He looked out the lobby doors to where his dad climbed into his car and slammed the door so hard we could hear it inside over all the noise. "In a year or two," he added as he followed his dad.

Mr. Taylor wasn't too pleased that he was left to deal with the aftermath by himself. "We are committed to offering sports to all members of our community," he said, wiping his forehead with his other sleeve. "This meeting has been called to find the best use of ice time, including providing more arena staff to be accessible more hours of the day, and working with schools to coordinate schedules and spares for students so as to allow for early afternoon practices. I have a proposal here, er, back in my office, that lays it all out."

Sister Kate, standing off to the side, gave a little cough into her hand and smiled.

"What about the girls?" I asked, finally finding my voice.

Mr. Taylor paled. He glanced around as if looking for reinforcements, but Mr. Russell was nowhere to be seen. A microphone was inches from his lips and the reporter had that 'eager for a story' look on her face. Coach Helen and her roommates were standing off to the side, their hands folded in front of them, gazing at him intently like they were going to start praying for his soul.

He looked just like the raccoon that had tried to escape our neighbour's German Shepherd by running into our shed and having the door slam shut behind him. They both knew the game was up, but they were pretty sore about it.

"The girls' end of season will be rescheduled once we contact the other teams."

We cheered. Mark's camera panned back and forth capturing our celebration.

After a round of high-fives and hugs, Rachel called over to Tyler.

"I guess you're sorry now that you showed up? Our bet seems to still be on."

Tyler laughed. "I really don't think we have to worry. The Roadrunners would have to win almost every game left in the season to even catch up to us. We're already voting on what kind of outfit you gals will be wearing."

"I wouldn't be placing an order quite yet," I said, trying to sound confident.

Tyler grinned and walked away.

"So, girls. Can I say how proud I am of you?" Helen said, coming over to us. "Peaceful demonstration can be a powerful thing."

"That and a little media pressure," said Rachel, grinning.

"Do you think we can get all our games in before the end of the season?" I asked.

"I'll be calling the other coaches tonight and we'll work something out, but it may be hectic."

"'Hectic' we can do," I said, watching the guys jostle and smack each other while looking over at us, jeering. "'Give up', we can't."

"Good attitude, girls." Helen smiled. "Well, I'll get going and start making those calls."

"Attitude, schmattitude," I said after she left. "I just do *not* want to see what my butt looks like in spandex."

There was a shuddering agreement all around me.

twenty-three

Coach Helen was as good as her word. By the next morning we all had an email giving us the new "hectic" schedule. Six games crammed into eleven days. Ouch. I was just glad that first semester exams were over, otherwise I don't know how we could have managed it.

Rachel and I bent our heads into the icy blast of a particularly nasty February wind.

"How close are we to catching up to the guys in the standings?" Rachel asked from behind her scarf.

I tried to get my brain to thaw. "With our win against the storm team..."

"The Tornadoes."

"...and the soggy team..."

"The Saugeen Stingrays."

"...and a tie against the yellow team, we're still sitting in third in our league," I said smugly. "The guys won their last few games and only have one left. They've moved up to second. We still have a chance. If we win every game," I added.

"We play a double header, or whatever you call it in hockey, against the Vipers in Petrolia next," Rachel said.

"The who?"

"The snake team. You know, with the Growler."

"That's OK," I said. "I'm ready for her."

"Yeah," Rachel said, with a glint in her eye. "A quick rabies shot and I'm good to go."

We were pretty hyper by the time we all met in the Petrolia arena dressing room.

At least we wouldn't have the added pressure today of the guys there. They probably would have gotten a ride to watch us but they had their own game to play against the Eagles in Julian Falls.

"Sam! For Pete's sake, just get dressed!" Andrea said after she accidentally knocked Sam's left shoulder pad as she stepped over all the equipment on the floor. Sam was taking everything off to start over.

"Easy there, Andrea," I said. "Why are you so wound up? Sam'll be ready in time." I looked over at Sam who was sitting very still with her eyes closed.

"Wound up? Didn't you see what they sent us?" Andrea grabbed a sheet of paper from her hockey bag and thrust it in my hands.

It was a picture off the Internet of a model wearing a skimpy cheerleading outfit. By skimpy I mean a skin-tight tank top with a deep 'V' neck so short it barely reached the model's rib cage. The bottoms were hip-hugger short-shorts. The girl in the picture was so excited to practically not be wearing any clothes that she was jumping in mid-air with a big toothy smile.

"Did you see what they wrote on the bottom?" Andrea asked. "*Hope to see you soon.*"

"If we don't beat the guys, I'm going to have to move out of Cartwright," Jenna said glumly, peering at the picture over my shoulder. "My dad would kill me if I ever wore something like that."

"They're just trying to get into our heads," Rachel said. "All we have to do is play like we know we can."

"And try not to get bitten," I muttered.

Sam was finally ready. We followed her out of the dressing room onto the ice.

We hit the ice flying. Our adrenaline kicked in and we tore up the rink. We scored two goals in the first period and held the snake team off for the rest of the game. We were feeling pretty cocky. One game down, one to go.

We spent our break between games laughing and joking. Things were going our way. We didn't push too hard in our warm-up. After all, we knew how to take this team. The puck dropped and our second game got under way.

Twenty minutes later we slunk back to the bench—down one to nothing. That one goal really ticked us off, too. Andrea got a penalty on a bad tripping call. It was obvious to everyone and their grandmother that Growler took a dive. Andrea had her stick on the other side of her after a backhand shot when Growler went down. Rachel tried to explain to the ref that it was impossible for Andrea to have tripped her, but Growler was rolling on the ice clutching her ankle in fake pain.

The ref simply waved Rachel off. It was just the break the snakes were waiting for. They managed to poke the puck in under Sam's pads during a scramble in front of the net.

Growler-girl made a miraculous recovery and was back on the ice before the period was over.

"It's stuff like this makes me wonder why we ever bothered to fight to finish our season," Lilly grumbled, wiping the sweat from her face.

"Good period, ladies," Coach Helen said, as we gathered around her along the boards. "I like the way you're battling. I want to see some solid passing this period, though. You were giving the puck away too many times, and this team is too strong to make mistakes around. OK, let's show them what we're made of."

Coach Helen beamed at us as we broke up the huddle.

"Not a word about that bogus penalty and how we were robbed?' Andrea sputtered as the first group of us skated back toward centre ice. "A 'good period'? How was that a good period?"

"Maybe she's taken a vow of 'positive attitude', too." Rachel said, angrily snapping her helmet strap on. "Does she always have to be so, so, happy?"

"I have to confess, I have this fantasy about her losing her temper someday and swearing at someone," Lilly said. "My dad said that before she became a nun, she could swear like a trucker."

"Now *that's* something I'd pay to hear," Sam said.

"Hey, does anyone know how the Hornets are doing?"

Jenna asked. "I've got this bad feeling."

I didn't like the sound of that.

"I could text my cousin at the end of the period," Andrea said. "I know she'll be at the game."

"Do it," I said. "If they're losing, it will buy us some breathing room." I was really feeling the pressure. After all, if the Hornets won, there was no way we could catch up in the league standings even if we won both this and our last game. The Hornets would finish first in their league and the best we could manage was second.

Another goal for the Vipers and none for us. This time they scored when our net had come off and Sam was trying to signal the ref to show him.

We argued the goal. The snake girls smirked. And the ref waved us off again.

"How much do you think they're paying him?" Rachel asked me, plunking herself down on the bench.

"Him, who?" I asked.

"The ref. This is obviously a fixed game."

"I don't know how much, but by the looks of him, he's paid in donuts."

"We can't lose this game," Rachel said. Her voice carried to the other girls on the bench. "I won't give the guys the satisfaction of being right."

The text reply from Andrea's cousin came in just before we headed back out to the ice at the end of the second break. It did nothing to relieve our feeling of doom.

2 to 1 for Hornets. End of 2nd.

Determination alone carried us through the third period. We put two in their net to end the game in a tie. Sister Helen was ecstatic with our effort. We were devastated.

Rachel and I got a ride back with Sam's mom, and although she chatted away about how proud she was of us, we said nothing. We knew that it was almost certain we had lost the bet. We hadn't had another text from Andrea's cousin. She probably didn't want to give us the bad news. And the guys were probably already placing an Internet order for outfits. How would the women of Cartwright feel when they saw us shaking our stuff at the Hornets games?

"There is a small chance that this isn't over," Sam said to us quietly. "Remember when we went to watch the Hornets play against the Eagles? They're the one team they hadn't beaten all season."

Rachel shook her head. "They had the momentum of winning the last game they played against them. And they were leading after two periods. The guys would have been totally pumped knowing it was their last game of the season and they were about the win the bet."

I had to agree with Rachel. "I think we have to face defeat," I said. "Andrea's cousin would have let us know if we had won. No text. No chance."

twenty-four

I didn't even turn on my computer at home. I didn't want to read any gloating emails from the guys or moaning emails from my team. I didn't know how I was going to face going to school the next morning. I wouldn't even have had to fake a sickness to stay home, either. Just the thought of the jeering and teasing we would take from the guys was enough to give me a real stomach ache.

I met Rachel partway to school since there was no talking my mom into letting me stay home. She took one look at me and said my stomach was bad because I hadn't eaten breakfast, and to get my tush out the door before she walked me to school like a kindergartner. I never get away with anything.

"Ready for the firing squad?" Rachel asked me, her mouth in a grim line.

"So, they won for sure, then?" I asked her.

"I guess so. I didn't hear any different. Mind you, I went to bed early."

"I'm surprised there aren't banners across the front door announcing it to the whole student body," I said, climbing the stairs to the front door as quickly as I could to escape the bitter cold.

Lilly found me at my locker. "Wasn't that great news about the Hornets?" she asked, beaming.

"What news?"

"They didn't win!"

"Where did you hear that?" I asked, afraid to believe it.

"Didn't you check your email?" Lilly asked. "I forwarded you the message Andrea got from her cousin. Her phone battery died in the third period so she couldn't call or text. She emailed the news when she got home."

"I can't believe they didn't beat the Eagles!"

"Well, they didn't actually lose, either. They tied so that means they ended in second place in their league. We're back two points from the team ahead of us in ours. We still have a chance. All we have to do is win our last game and finish second, just like them. And they said a tie would go to us."

Hope surged once again. "Who do we play for our last game?" I asked.

"The Greys."

I tried to think back. "Which ones were they?"

"Orange shirts," Lilly called over her shoulder, heading to art class.

Hope faded again. I couldn't help wishing it was an easier team. On the other hand, we'd improved so much with Coach Helen. Plus, it was the Greys/oranges game that made us want to find a new coach and get back into the league. So maybe it was fitting.

My passing had been sloppy lately and I thought I should get some pointers before our last game. I stood at the side of the pond for a good two minutes before Kip noticed me. He seemed pretty intent on destroying the back of the net with slapshots. When he finally saw me, he gave a little chin raise and went to retrieve the pucks while I laced up.

"Sooo," I said. "How are things?"

"How do you think?" He unceremoniously dumped the pucks on the ice and took a few more violent shots.

"That good, huh?"

He stopped shooting and leaned on his stick. "Well, let's see. My dad isn't talking to me because of what I said to the reporter at the meeting. My mom isn't talking to me because I've upset my dad. My coach isn't talking to me because my dad fired him after our performance last night, and none of the guys are talking to each other, either."

I didn't know what to say. "I'm really sorry, Kip."

"What are you sorry for?"

"Well, I kinda pushed you to stand up to your dad, and now look..."

"You know what? It needed to be done. I'm actually glad I'm not dancing around the issue with him anymore. He'll just have to deal with it."

I had to admit, a backbone looked good on the guy. In fact, he looked good all over.

"So, you want to help me with some passing drills?" I said lamely, hoping he wouldn't see the blush spreading across my cheeks.

"No."

I looked up quickly.

"That's not want I want to do at all." His eyes locked on mine and I barely registered that he had let go of his stick and dropped his gloves. He put his hands on either side of my face and pulled me to him. Then he kissed me. I felt warmth spread right down to my toes curling inside my skates.

He pulled back as if to check my reaction. My goofy grin must have given him his answer because he moved his arms down around my back and kissed me again.

Clearly, my passing skills weren't going to get any attention.

I couldn't believe how many people turned out for the game. It was nothing compared to the guys, but we were still pretty excited. I gave a quick wave over to Dolores and George. I knew they were pulling for us. But I think a lot of the crowd were friends of the Hornets and would be cheering for the other team.

I don't remember the warm-up or Coach Helen's pep talk in the dressing room. It was like someone had snapped their fingers and I was crouched in position, waiting for the ref to drop the puck.

The first two periods were like a bad game of tag. We'd get control of the puck, they'd steal it from us. We'd snatch it back, they'd grab it. Back and forth and back and forth with neither team managing to get more than a few weak shots on goal.

"Good game so far, ladies," Coach Helen said on the break before the third period. "I like how you're fighting for control and staying out of the penalty box. And you know, even a tie game here will give us home ice advantage in the playoffs."

"A tie is as good as a loss when it comes to spandex," Rachel said.

"Do you mean the bet? Is it that close?" Coach Helen asked.

Several of us nodded.

"Listen, you need to play the game for yourselves and not worry about the outcome. You girls have terrific energy as a team and it's a team effort that will win this." She paused and looked at our troubled faces. "Do you mean just tight-fitting outfits or truly spandex?"

Andrea pulled out the flyer again.

Coach Helen paled. "Oh," she said and looked up. "Girls, you need a goal and you need it bad."

We all nodded, grabbed our gear, and headed out to the bench.

The third period was when things started to go wrong. I don't know whether it was the pressure of knowing we had to win, or if it was just that we had played flat-out for forty minutes already and were tired, but whatever the reason, we were making mistakes.

Only a few minutes in and we had already lost the puck three times on turnovers. If Sam hadn't made some spectacular saves, we'd be practising our high kicks already.

"Andrea, make sure someone is free before you pass the puck," Rachel snapped at her as we skated back to the bench after a whistle for offside.

"I did!" Andrea snarled back. "But that human tanker truck there keeps blocking my shots."

We plunked ourselves on the wooden bench and watched the action while leaning over the boards and trying to catch our breath. Deb and Kayla were frantically trying to clear the puck out of our end as Sam skated back and forth in the crease trying to keep her eyes on it. The Greys' number 3 was in front and took a shot. As Sam put up her blocker, another Grey sideswiped her and knocked her to the ground just as we heard the clink of the puck hitting the post.

We listened expectantly for the whistle to call goaltender interference, but none came. We looked at Coach Helen with shocked faces—that was clearly a penalty. Coach Helen yelled to the referee but he turned his back and ignored her.

The clock was ticking down. We only had about three minutes left to score. The whistle blew and the ref signaled icing against our team.

Rachel, Andrea, and I hopped the boards to join Lilly and Jenna on the ice for the line change.

Rachel took the face-off and I was behind her by the boards. She gave me a quick nod before getting into her crouch. That meant that if she got the puck, she wasn't even going to keep it on her stick but bounce it right to me.

There was a blur of sticks and then suddenly the puck was in front of me. I grabbed it and took off for enemy territory. Number 16 was hot on my trail, her stick jabbing at me as she tried to knock the puck away. Rachel was on my right so I passed to her and took up a spot near the blue line to snag the puck and keep it in their zone if it got loose. Jenna and number 16 were both in front of the net. The Greys' player was trying to shove her out of the way, but Jenna spread her legs a bit and stood firm. As Rachel and number 7 fought for the puck along the boards, I saw number 16 give Jenna a huge shove from behind and send her sprawling headfirst into their goalie.

A whistle blew. That orange shirt deserved the penalty she was about to get.

"Blue—number 11, goaltender interference."

I had heard wrong. I was sure of it. How could *we* be getting the penalty?

Jenna's expression alternated between shock and rage as she was escorted to the penalty box. The Three Stooges, in their usual spot behind the sin bin, were yelling at the ref as he talked to the scorekeeper, but we knew it was no use. The call stood.

The others skated over to me.

"Tell me we're not going to be shorthanded for the last

two minutes of a tied game," Rachel said.

Oh, how I wished I could. This was the worst thing that could happen. Not only were we down a player, but the fact that it was a bad call made us feel like we'd been sucker-punched. Coach Helen called a time-out.

"Just look at them over there gloating," Lilly said, when we had gathered by the bench.

The Greys were grinning behind their masks. I could just imagine the red starting to creep up Rachel's neck. One minute, thirty-seven seconds left in the game.

"OK, team," Coach Helen said, "this is a rotten time for a penalty, but let's just focus on killing it off. Make sure you ice that puck as much as possible. Anytime it comes *near* your stick, send it hard down the other end."

The buzzer sounded and we headed back for the face-off. The puck dropped and both sides fought for control. Their captain managed to get it on her stick and quickly passed it to her teammate on the other side. Well, she *tried* to pass it to her. As the puck slid across the ice, Rachel lunged forward and knocked the puck out to centre ice. I burst forward and snagged it, and took off for the Greys' net. Rachel saw the turnover and skated hard behind me.

As I came down the ice, their goalie slid forward, ready for my shot.

I made like I was going to shoot, but passed it to Rachel instead. The goalie pivoted to face Rachel, who quickly fired it back to me. I pulled my arm back, transferred my weight, hit the puck, rolled my wrists, and held my breath as the puck flew...

"I never thought I'd say this," Sam said, gliding beside me. "But it feels good to be back on the ice."

I nodded, feeling my blades biting into the surface, sending me surging forward. Sam headed to the net and I took my position at centre ice, waiting for the puck drop.

I looked up to see my mom and dad in the stands, warming their hands on coffee cups, here for our opening game of the new season. And because we had a prime weekend afternoon ice slot, Dolores and George hired their two nieces to work the bakery so they could come.

And there, in the seats behind our bench was the entire Hornets team, leaning forward in the seats with their elbows on their knees, laughing and joking with each other. Three of them were particularly familiar; they looked remarkably like the Three Stooges only with their faces painted in our team colours. Kip had even painted my number—45—on his right cheek.

I don't know what made me smile the most—the turnout at the game, the chance to take another run at our league championship under Coach Helen, or fact that every last one of the Hornets was wearing a Roadrunner jersey and waving blue and white pompoms.

Overtime

For more real-life Hockey Girl stories, go to our website:
www.fitzhenry.ca/HockeyGirl